'82 MYSTERY

*To Seven
Pleasure working
with you!*

A Novel

R.M. Wood

R.M. Wood

82Mystery.com

DISCLAIMER

This is a work of fiction. Names, characters, places, and incidents either are the product of the author's imagination or are used fictitiously, and any resemblance to actual persons living or dead, business establishments, events, or locales is entirely coincidental.

To Grandma

PROLOGUE

May 18, 1982

THE tall, thin, 16-year-old boy with curly brown hair sauntered across the street. He knocked on the door of a well-maintained older house. An elderly woman opened the door and invited him in.

The house was around the corner from a four story apartment building that was next to the water. TWILIGHT TOWERS was the name on the sign.

The boy sat on the sofa, and the woman served him a plate of her homemade chocolate chip cookies. He helped himself.

"Thanks, Grandma. Mmm! These are delicious!"

She smiled. "So, how's school?"

"Pretty good."

"What about your girl?"

"Oh, she's fine."

"You know, Rick, yesterday a young girl either jumped or fell from Twilight Towers. They took her to the hospital, but I think she died."

He froze. Only minutes before he had passed that building.

Then a strange feeling came over him. It was the strangest, most powerful feeling of Déjà vu he had ever had in his life. In his mind, he saw *two* girls on a balcony at Twilight Towers, not one. And he got the feeling that there was more to what happened than anyone knew.

The next day, while doing his afternoon paper route, the 16-year-old boy read the news story about the girl who fell. It wasn't on the front page, but buried on Page 8.

1

The story was vague and mysterious. The pieces didn't add up. How does someone just fall from a balcony? There was very little information.

He began to imagine how it happened. Did she commit suicide? Did she think she could fly after taking LSD?

One of his classmates had died three months before. He took LSD one night and jumped out a window, thinking he could fly. Some doctor even had a name for it: "Chemically Induced Flight Syndrome."

Still reading the news story, the 16-year-old boy realized the date the girl fell. He gasped in open-mouth horror, dropping his newspaper bag. The papers spilled over the sidewalk.

He knew that date well. He would never forget it.

Suddenly, he knew what happened. For a moment, he saw into the future.

Looking across the water, he could see Twilight Towers. It was a four story building, with rounded arch openings on the front porches, shaped like horseshoes.

Though he barely noticed the building before, looking at it then scared the hell out of him. It was a strange fear, one that he couldn't quite understand. It was like an omen. A sense of foreboding, like something evil was hiding in the building that he couldn't see.

But he wouldn't see that evil until many, many years later.

ONE

It was a tragic chain of events.

SHE rolled down Cherry Hill Lane. On a hilly, green street she rode. On a bicycle with a freezer box in front and an umbrella on top.

She brought happiness with her when she rang her bell and people stopped her to buy their favorite ice cream treat. Everybody called her 'Ice Cream Girl.'

It was a small town by the sea. The town was picturesque on a summer day -- Ocean Bay, Massachusetts.

She wore a white uniform: White shoes, socks, shorts, shirt, and a white cap with a black visor.

'SHELLY'S ICE CREAM' it said on front of the cart, with a crude logo of a girl resembling her. That made sense. Her name was Michelle.

She tied her long brown hair into a ponytail or pigtails.

Sometimes she carried a kaleidoscope swirl lollipop.

Some people said she was Native American, or part Native American. Actually, she was French Canadian, and she had brown, almond-shaped eyes.

She was short, lithe, and thin. Possibly 5'4'' tall, maybe 105 pounds soaking wet.

They say she was a schoolteacher once. 6th Grade English. That was two years ago.

One of the parents said Michelle's students always scored the highest on their state reading tests. She did this by having the kids act out the stories they read. They seemed to like that. Jumping up on the desks and running around the classroom. Using broom handles as swords.

Someone even wrote about her in a magazine.

Then she quit teaching. No one knew why. But there were rumors.

One rumor was that she had a nervous breakdown. Another rumor was that she had an affair with a parent. Yet another rumor was that she assaulted a student and they forced her to resign.

Some people thought she sold drugs from her ice cream bike. Can you believe that?

At the end of the day, or when she ran out of ice cream, she went back to a house by the water that had a three car garage. That was where they parked a Mercedes and a Corvette.

But one summer there was no ice cream girl. That summer ended suddenly. Something went terribly wrong.

There is only one person who knows the story from beginning to end. That person talked to everybody. That person knew what was on the ice cream girl's mind. They talked many times.

It was a tragic chain of events. It really was. Not everybody agrees on all the events or the details, but everybody agrees on the gist of the story.

Well, here it is. Maybe by telling it, something like this won't happen to you, or someone you care about.

TWO

"Oysters in a sandbox, that is what they are!"

THE ice cream girl glided down the hill on her bike. She was racing against time. She had to get to the school. It was time for school to get out, and today was almost 80 degrees! Warm for May, but sometimes you get that in New England.

When she got to the school, the place was alive with activity. Students streamed out the doors, getting on the buses or into their waiting parents' cars.

She rang her bell.

"Mom! Can I get an ice cream?" yelled a girl.

"The ice cream girl's here!" yelled a boy.

"She used to be a teacher here! Mrs. M!" said another boy, waving to her.

They formed a line.

"A Strawberry Shortcake, please!"

"Lemon-Lime Shots!"

"Chocolate Éclair!"

"Drumstick!"

Then there were only three people left in line. It was the principal, Mr. Kinecki, and Sarah and Ashley, two of Michelle's former students. Now they were in 8th Grade.

"We miss you here, Michelle!" said Mr. Kinecki.

Ever since she first met Mr. Kinecki, Michelle thought there was something very familiar about him. She had seen him before. But where? She could never figure it out. But it made her uncomfortable.

The wind blew his sandy hair that he had combed over his otherwise bald head. His face was blotchy and his eyes were glazed.

He bought a Toasted Almond bar.

5

"You can always come back," he said. "I don't understand this ice cream thing."

Sarah and Ashley giggled their way up to the front.

"Hi, Mrs. M.!" said Sarah. "Could I please have a Watermelon Bomb Pop?"

Ashley got an Orange Cream Bar.

Sarah was short and thin with light brown hair and a whiny voice. She always wanted attention, much like a friendly, playful, kitten.

Ashley was taller and more built with long black hair, green eyes, rosy cheeks, and light freckles. *She reminded Michelle of Holly.* NO! STOP! Michelle couldn't think of Holly right now. Everything was going so well.

As Michelle waited on the girls, there was certain uneasiness in the air. *Would the girls ever forgive her for what happened?*

They giggled off, jostling each other in friendly horseplay.

Michelle's next stop was the police station, by the park, near the sea, where she had several regular customers. One of them was Megan, a pretty young police officer with big brown eyes, and light brown hair with blonde highlights.

Megan always got a Starburst fruit pop.

"Guess what, Michelle," said Megan. "I just got promoted! I'm an investigator now!"

Michelle smiled. "Congratulations!"

"So, how do you keep this thing cold?" asked Megan.

"Cold plates. You plug it in at night and the freezer runs. And the plates stay cold for eight to twelve hours."

Michelle sold even more at the park. That's when she saw it.

At the far end of the park was the entrance to the woods. That's where The Caves were.

There was an area in that town deep within the woods where there was a high granite rock cliff that the kids called "The Caves." It was about a half a mile in the woods and the terrain was so rough and thickly wooded that no car or off-road vehicle could even get through. And it was hard to find, unless you were very familiar with it, especially in the dark with no lights. Hence, it made a perfect place for those notorious teenage drinking parties.

The Caves were high, almost four stories, with many levels and areas where you could hide anyone or anything. *If only you could hide your worse memories there forever.*

Michelle remembered when she used to go there back in 1982, when she was a teenager. Wow. 1982. What a year it was. It was a time of great change. There were the parties. There were the drugs. There was Holly. Holly. Why, it was Holly who took her to The Caves for the first time. You couldn't go alone, not if you didn't know anybody there. You couldn't find it unless someone took you there. And you might not get back if you weren't with someone. If you were a girl, you had to be careful of some of the boys . . .

There was that incident many years ago, when Mr. Kinecki's own son Billy had fallen from The Caves and died. There was so little information about it. No one saw him fall. Apparently, he was drinking.

Michelle had to stop thinking about it.

The later it got, the more the sky turned dark. Black clouds rolled in. Then the thunder and lightning started.

Michelle raced home on her bike, put it in the garage, and plugged the freezer in.

She started the Mercedes that was parked in the garage and drove out of the driveway.

The rain came down in sheets. Michelle turned her windshield wipers up all the way. The wiper blades threw the water off in cascades.

She had to get home to her husband Rick, in time to make dinner. Or maybe they would go out, since it was Friday. But she wanted to see that building first.

She turned the corner and there it stood in the fading light. She was looking at a four story apartment building that stood by the water next to The Periwinkle restaurant.

Dim green lights lit the porches. Curved arch openings gave the balconies light, shaped like – like caves. How many times had she driven by this building in the last twenty years and thought about it? How many times had she thought about – about Holly?

Michelle parked the car down the street and walked through the rain. People with umbrellas passed her, shivering. She walked the whole length of the building and looked up to the fourth floor.

Michelle thought she could hear music coming from inside the building. Melancholy music.

After awhile she could make out the singing: *"Oysters in a sandbox, that is what they are!"*

She couldn't remember the song or the artist, but the words were: *"There once was a time/When I was bad to you/There once was a time/When you were there for me/I fell from grace, you slipped away."*

Fell. Bad to you. What if anyone knew? What if anyone found out what happened there in 1982? If Rick ever found out, it would destroy him. If the police ever found out . . . prison. Wait! That was in 1982! It wouldn't matter anyway! She was older and wiser. She had her teaching certificate. That would count for something, wouldn't it?

That building gave her the creeps, but she had to see it anyway. The building knew her secret. Holly didn't know anymore, because Holly was gone. Maybe it was time to remember Holly.

What would Holly be like today? Would she have kids at the school? What would her husband – or ex-husband be like? Would Holly be a difficult parent?

Michelle turned and walked back to her car.

The rain started to pour heavily.

From a fourth floor window, someone was watching her.

THREE

"Just a terrible accident."

EVEN though it was built forty years ago, the police station was clean and modern-looking, Megan thought. It had tan bricks and frosted, square windows. The American flag waved from the flagpole.

She pulled up in her new car, the one she bought when she found out she made detective.

She turned the engine off, looked in her rear-view mirror, and put lip gloss on. Wait! Was this appropriate? Did female detectives where lip gloss?

She reached into her purse for a tissue. Wait! Did female detectives carry purses?

She could always leave it in the car. After all, no one would dare break into a car to steal a purse that was parked at the police station, would they? Not unless it was another cop.

Megan took a brush from her glove compartment and brushed her long, wavy, light brown hair with the blonde high-lights. Pulling out a scrunchie, she tied her hair back in a bun.

Chief Marcus was waiting for her. He smiled.

"Detective Downs, got a minute?" he beckoned to the inside of his office.

"Congratulations!" said the Chief.

"Thanks." Megan blushed.

"Sit down!"

She did.

"There was sure a wide pool of applicants. Good people. A lot of people from other departments, out of town. You know how we have to advertise in the papers – town policy – no conflict of interest . . . but you know we try to pick someone from inside . . . and you have a mighty fine record . . ." he pointed to a manila folder.

" . . . always on time for work . . . always willing to work extra details . . . willing to go to court . . . now you've been here how long, Detective?"

"Oh, I started at the front desk when I was still in college. Five years, I guess?"

"Well, let's hope you'll be here thirty more. We like people to stay with us. Now you know the guy you're replacing . . . Sergeant Antonelli . . . great guy . . ."

Megan cringed when she heard the name Sergeant Antonelli.

The Chief kept babbling: "Guess he's thinking about moving to Florida now that he's retiring . . . well anyway, you know what my command is like. I let folks work their own way with their own style. As long as work gets done, gets done right, I'm a happy man. I've read some of your reports. Fine police reports. Fine writing."

Megan's big brown eyes wandered around his office as he rambled on.

The Chief stopped talking.

There was a long, uncomfortable silence.

"You know, Detective Downs, Megan, can I call you Megan?"

She nodded.

"I know how hard it can be starting a new position. Don't let the fact that you're the first female detective in this department make you uncomfortable. Don't forget, I was the first black . . . ah . . . African American here years ago . . ." he rambled on about how a police officer was a police officer no matter what. How times had changed and people were different now . . .

Her mind began to wander. Would she have the same experiences she had as a uniformed officer? The ones that made her want to get up in the morning and go to work? Like when she got that call to respond to a possible drowning. Two 8-year-old boys were watching waves crash against the seawall after a storm. One boy got up on the wall for a better look. He lost his balance fell into the wild sea.

When Megan got there, she drove her cruiser over the curb, onto the grass of the park, knocked over a barrel, and stopped by the wall.

A crowd had gathered and the boy's father was there, screaming, crying, and frantically walking the length of the pier.

"MY SON! MY SON! OH GOD, NO! He can't swim!"

Huge waves crashed over the wall, splashing him. But getting wet on that cold day was the last thing on his mind.

He looked into her eyes as if she were the last person alive on earth after the Apocalypse.

If Megan had thought about it, she wouldn't have done it.
She knew that now.

She took off her utility belt and shoes, tossing them into the front seat of her car. Then she ran to the steps, where waves were hitting so hard that they had knocked cement blocks out.

Megan looked and looked, but couldn't see any sign of the boy.

Suddenly, in the trough of a wave, she saw brown hair and a small hand sticking up.

In she dove. The waves pushed her to and fro.

She did the butterfly stroke. And she timed the waves. When a peak came at her, she dove under it.

She lost sight of the boy. Where was he?

Wait! Were those fingers sticking up? She swam towards them.

It was the boy, sunk just below her. She grabbed him and pulled his head to the surface.

He didn't look good. No color.

Then a wave foamed over them and Megan lost her grip. The boy began to sink.

She dove deep, grabbing at anything. She got nothing.

Megan ran out of air, so she resurfaced, gasping for breath. Her whole body was numb from the cold and she had trouble keeping her head above water.

She dove again, reaching for anything. Her fingers grabbed something. Hair? Seaweed? No, it was hair! She lost her grip.

She dove one more inch, grabbing the hair with her right hand, and then what must have been his jacket with her left.

Megan fought with all her might to find daylight above. They broke the water's surface.

The boy's wet clothes made it hard to keep him afloat. If she could just keep his head up . . .

Megan heard the whir of a small engine. She waved her free hand.

The fire department rescue boat brushed up beside them. They pulled Megan and the boy onto the deck.

The paramedics began CPR immediately.

The boat sped to the dock.

They airlifted him to the hospital.

For the next two days, the boy fought for his life in ICU. But he survived, with no permanent injuries.

One day she responded to a report of a theft. When she got to the house, a family, Mom, Dad, and two young children, a boy and a girl, were frantic. Someone had stolen Willy, their beloved dog.

"How do you know he was *stolen*?" asked Megan.

The girl had seen Willy in the window of a house several blocks away. She knew it was him. Willy wore a red leather collar and a blue dog bone ID tag.

Megan rang the doorbell of the house. The eaves were rotting and the house needed a new coat of paint. The overgrowth of grass and bushes had already consumed the walkway, and the driveway was next.

No answer. Maybe the doorbell didn't work. Megan knocked.

The woman who answered was in her mid 80's. She reminded Megan of her grandmother, who rested in peace.

They talked, or mostly the elderly woman did. She had found a new lease on life! She took in a stray dog . . .

Megan was delicate but firm.

"But he's a seeing-eye dog Ma'am!" she said. "Highly trained. The blind man thought he closed the door, but the dog got out . . . hard for the guy . . . has trouble walking . . ."

She hated to lie. But she hated to break the woman's heart even more.

The old woman broke down in tears and apologized profusely. Megan put Willy in the backseat of her cruiser.

"Could you find my dog?" the woman cried. "She disappeared ages ago . . . I can't drive anymore . . ."

"I'll try Ma'am. I'll try."

A happy reunion between family and dog came to pass. Everybody cried; even the father. Willy wagged his tail and tried to kiss everybody. Megan felt a tear run down her cheek.

Back at the station, Megan made a call to the animal shelter.

"We have a litter of puppies," said the girl on the phone, "but you better get here quick! They're going fast! Awfully cute!"

"I need a *special* dog, for my grandmother," said Megan.

The girl sighed. "Well, we have an older dog. Very gentle. Very loving. Small dog. A Fox Terrier. But she's old. Probably 11 or 12. Nobody wants her. It's so sad. They'll have to put her down in a couple of days . . ."

Megan brought the Fox Terrier to the elderly woman's house. The woman answered the door.

"I think I found your dog Ma'am . . ."

The dog wagged her tail. The elderly woman bent down and patted her; instant friends.

The woman burst into tears. She hugged Megan.

"Thank you! Thank you so much!" cried the woman.

Megan lugged in the big bag of dog food, treats, dog toys, leash, collar, and dog license. The woman kept crying and thanking her.

Would her new detective job give her memories like those?

When Chief Marcus finished rambling, she got up to leave.

". . . oh, there's one more thing . . ." he said. "Years ago, that kid who got killed in the woods . . ."

Megan wanted to cry, but instead she forced a smile.

"Just a terrible accident." She heard herself say. "We were just a bunch of stupid kids who couldn't hold our liquor. We shouldn't have been drinking. I made a statement about that at the time, which I'm sure you've read."

He nodded. "Then we don't have to talk about it anymore. Sorry I brought it up."

So was she.

He handed her a folder. There a picture of a heavy-set, muscular man on the front. He had curly brown hair and blue eyes with a sleepy, slanted, cowboy look to them. His face sported a mustache and goatee. The rest of his face was unshaven with razor stubble.

"What's this?" asked Megan.

"Just some junk mail I get from time to time. This guy's an investigative hypnotist. Used to work for the U.S. Marshals. We'll probably never need an investigative hypnotist, but just keep it on file for now."

Megan looked at the picture again. The guy was hot!

Megan closed the door to her one bedroom apartment. She took the holster and handcuffs off her hips. Then she took off the badge that she wore as a necklace. She laid them all down on the counter.

She looked at her cell phone. No new messages. No missed calls. Megan sighed.

Walking into the clean, neat kitchen, she pulled a plate out of the cabinet. She took a piece of leftover pizza from the refrigerator, put it on the plate and put it in the microwave.

So Megan ate her pizza. Then she watched *Thelma and Louise* with her cat, Kit Kat, on her lap. He was a grey and black striped male tabby with tortoise shell markings on his belly.

When the movie was over she dangled yarn and Kit Kat tried to catch it with his paws.

Then she looked at her Teddy Bear collection, all thirty of them. She had set them up on the window seat. The window that looked out into the alley, that no one could see in.

She looked at the folder of the investigative hypnotist, which she had brought home with her. His name was Dunn. No last name. Or was that his last name?

He had a website.

She logged onto her computer and onto his website. She clicked on an icon and a video started to play. It was Dunn talking about why he became an investigative hypnotist.

As she listened, she became mesmerized. She couldn't take her eyes away from the screen.

Dunn told a sad story about what had happened to his father, and why he went into law enforcement. It was to protect the innocent and to get to the truth, always. Megan felt a tear run down her cheek.

She could relate to Dunn. Especially after what happened.

FOUR

". . . . yesterday a young girl either jumped or fell from Twilight Towers. . . ."

THE orange and red sun set over the sleepy sea and twilight appeared. Michelle rolled home with her money box tucked under her arm. She put the ice cream bike in the garage and plugged the freezer in. It roared like a lion when it started.

Opening it, she counted the ice cream. Oh, no; almost out of Oreo Bars.

She strode into the kitchen, dropped the money box on the breakfast counter, and pulled up a stool. Her husband, Rick, came in and kissed her. He was tall and thin, with curly brown hair and a moustache and beard.

"So, how was it?" he asked.

"Tiring. But I made a lot of money. How's the real estate game?"

"I finally leased out Cumberland Street again, and we did the inspection on the ten units in Rumford. They'll need work. But the cash flow will be good. Someone's got to pay the bills around here!"

"Oh, stop!" Michelle rubbed her elongated oval-shaped eyes. She stretched her lithe, petite body.

"You know," said Rick, "I've never seen you so happy! You really love this ice cream gig! When you were teaching you were always stressed out! Now you can work with kids and you don't have to tell them to sit down and be quiet."

Michelle winced. "I hated that!"

A song was playing on the stereo in the background. Michelle started to listen to it. The singers sang: *". . . Tripping down the streets of the city/Flying high with rainbow eyes/She crashes on the*

15

sand with no disguise/Beach fun with Judy/Beach fun with Judy/Seasons with Judy . . ."

"What's that song about?" asked Michelle.

"Well, think about the words, tripping down the streets of the city, rainbow eyes, flying, crashing, – it's about a girl on LSD. *"Beach Fun With Judy. Judy* is a street name for LSD."

In her mind, Michelle saw a girl on the railing of a porch with her arms out wide, ready to jump. Her green eyes were glowing.

"Are you hungry?" asked Michelle.

Rick nodded.

"Let's go out to eat at The Periwinkle! My treat! I sold a lot of ice cream today!"

"Rick," said Michelle, after a sip of her wine. "You know a lot about music – what was that song – I think the words were: 'There once was a time when I was bad to you, there once was a time when you were there for me . . .'"

". . . I fell from grace," Rick joined in, ". . . you slipped away . . ."

"Yeah! That's it!"

Rick thought about it. "I think the tune was called *Oysters In A Sandbox.*"

"Yes! That's it."

"Why?"

"Oh, I heard it the other day."

"What's wrong with your wrist?" he touched it.

Michelle held it up. "Nothing. Why?"

"You're always twitching it."

The waitress put the check face down next to Rick. He passed it to Michelle.

"Today I met with Jimmy Jendron," said Rick, "one of my contractors . . ."

Michelle had never met Jimmy Jendron, but she always felt there was something very familiar about the name. She had heard it before. *Hearing that name gave her the same feeling she got about Mr. Kinecki.*

As they left the restaurant, Michelle looked up to the fourth floor of the building next door. The first unit, on the end, had its lights on.

"What's up there?" asked Rick.

"Oh, nothing. Rick, what do you know about this building?"

Rick shrugged. "I've always had a strange feeling about it. It kind of gives me the creeps, to be honest. I guess a long time ago it was a restaurant and seedy ocean front hotel. They used to call it The Twilight House. Then they added two floors and made it into apartments . . . calling it Twilight Towers after that . . . then, I think thirty years ago, they made it into condos."

"Oh."

"Why?"

"Would you ever think about converting an apartment building to condos?"

"Yeah. But a building like this would be too overpriced now . . . and it used to have a bad reputation. Plus, not that it matters, but it's an ugly building. It doesn't seem to fit in with any of the others . . ."

"What do you mean a bad reputation?"

"Well, I guess in the '80's there was a lot of partying going on here, a lot of drugs."

Michelle stopped walking.

"Are you alright?" asked Rick.

Michelle nodded. "What else have you heard about it?"

Rick scratched his head. "Actually, come to think of it . . ."

His mind went back to when he was a teenager, sitting in his grandmother's living room.

"You know, Rick, yesterday a young girl either jumped or fell from Twilight Towers . . ." his grandmother had said.

Then Rick remembered reading about it in the paper, as he did his afternoon paper route. They rushed the girl to the hospital. She died two days later.

He didn't know her.

"There was something very mysterious about it," he said. "I remember there wasn't very much information. I guess some people thought it was a suicide. At the time, I remember thinking that she might've taken LSD and jumped off thinking she could fly. That actually happened to a classmate of mine . . . Mark Fiore. He took LSD one night and jumped out a window."

17

Michelle shook her head.

"What was the girl's name who fell off the building -- Holly?"

Michelle gasped. Her mouth fell open.

"What's the matter?" asked Rick.

"I don't feel so good," she said. "It must've been something I ate."

"Yeah, you've got to be careful with seafood."

Although he tried, Rick couldn't sleep over the sound of the television. Why was it on? He drifted in and out of a stupor of half-sleep that allowed him to know what the people on TV were going to say before they said it. Finally, he sat up.

The room was dark. Michelle was sitting up in bed staring at the screen.

"Are you alright?" Rick asked. "How do you feel?"

Michelle's face was blank. Her cheeks were stained by tears.

"Oh, I'm alright. The Pepto Bismo helped me. Rick, there's something I have to tell you."

"Bad?"

"Well, yes and no." She sniffed and wiped her nose with a tissue.

"What is it?"

Michelle stared down. She covered her face.

"You've been crying! What happened?"

"I always cry, you know that!"

Rick didn't know what to say.

"You know we were talking about Twilight Towers . . ." she said. "And you mentioned that girl who fell from there back in '82 . . ."

"Yeah?"

"Well, I knew her. I used to hang around with her. She was my friend . . ." she sobbed.

Rick hugged her.

"Michelle, I'm sorry. You never told me about that."

"It was just too painful to remember. It was so long ago . . . then that song reminded me . . ."

"*Oysters In A Sandbox*?"

"Yes!"

"How did it happen? Did she jump? Did she fall by accident?"

Michelle was silent for what seemed like an eternity. Should she tell Rick? NO! He just wasn't ready to hear it. Not tonight anyway.

"I don't know! They never found out! I thought she was going to be alright, but she wasn't!"

"What was your friend like?"

"Well, she was older than my other friends because she had stayed back a couple of times. Really smart. But nobody knew it. She wouldn't do any work in school. Very pretty. Irish face with rosy cheeks, pretty green eyes, fair skin, and light freckles. She was built, and all the guys thought she was hot . . . She used to change the color of her hair all the time. She'd be bleach-blonde, then black-haired, then light brown, then red . . ."

"I'm sorry that happened to her. It sounds like she was a really good friend. You must've looked up to her."

"I did. Oh, I did."

But they were far from through with that conversation.

FIVE

"Holly is dead!"

LATER, Rick realized that the days that followed should've been a warning. Maybe he just couldn't face what was happening.

One of the first signs was that Michelle suddenly wanted him to call her 'Shelly.' He didn't see anything wrong with that.

Another portent was that she wanted to eat at The Periwinkle more and more. When they walked by, she would always look up to the fourth floor porch of Twilight Towers.

It was the hostess at The Periwinkle that got Michelle's attention at first, she told Rick later. The hostess had long black hair, a freckly face, and almond-shaped eyes. Her voice was whiny and nasal. She was tall and shapely.

Michelle kept turning her head towards the hostess. After awhile, she had trouble keeping her eyes off her.

At one point, the girl actually caught Michelle staring at her. The girl smiled politely. Michelle dropped her salad fork under the table.

"You okay?" asked Rick.

"Oh, ah, yeah, I guess." Michelle was dazed and disoriented.

She wiped her mouth, which was a turned down one and always made her look like she was frowning.

"Did the hostess say anything to you earlier? Do you know her from somewhere?"

"She didn't say anything . . . but I do feel like I know her from somewhere."

"Where?"

"I'll tell you later."

Michelle remembered. *It was May Day. They set up a Maypole in the park and kids were dancing around it with streamers.*

20

Michelle had "run away from home" after a fight with her mother. She was twelve years old.

Mad, crying, and tired, she wandered two streets over to the park across from the police station, and across from the Catholic Church. Her pigtails blowing in the wind, she sat down on a swing and tottered on it, making patterns in the sand with her worn out sneakers.

A short time later, a passing figure blocked her light. Looking up, she saw a girl with long black hair, freckles, and a womanly figure walk past. She was only a couple of years older than Michelle.

The girl had green eyes that danced all around and sized Michelle up. Her innocent face seemed to contradict the outfit she had on.

What caught Michelle's eyes the most was the cigarette the girl was puffing on.

Then the girl spoke to her: "Hey, little girl, you got a quarter? I need to make a phone call."

Michelle shook her head.

"I didn't think so!" the girl laughed.

Angry, Michelle blurted out: "Have you got a cigarette?"

The girl stopped laughing. "Like you've ever smoked one before!"

"Have, too!"

The girl chuckled again, and removed a pack from the pocket of her black pants. Her blouse, with low cleavage, was also black.

She handed Michelle a cigarette. Michelle put it between her fingers. The closest she had come to this was when she had snuck a cigarette from her Uncle Charlie's pack years ago. But she never had the nerve to light it up.

The girl took out a lighter and struck it. Michelle still held the cigarette.

"Well?" said the girl. "Are you going to put it in your mouth or what?"

Michelle did. The girl lit the cigarette.

Michelle sucked it in to her feet. Then she turned green, her eyes watered, and she started to cough. She felt nauseous and she doubled over with her head on her knees.

This was more than the older girl could take. She started to laugh hysterically, slapping her thighs.

"So, you've smoked before?" she laughed.

21

Michelle was too overwhelmed to speak at first. Finally, she coughed, ". . . please . . . help . . . me . . ."

Ten minutes later, after Michelle took a drink of water from the fountain, helped to her feet by her new acquaintance, she asked the girl: "What's your name?"

"Holly."

Michelle would see Holly around town. At the convenience store. On the bus. At the mall. And sometimes when their eyes met they would nod to each other.

Michelle wished she could have a friend like Holly. Someone who was carefree and not afraid to be a little different. Her best friend, Lauren, thought clothes were the most important thing in life. Michelle wished she could have new clothes from the mall every week like Lauren. But Michelle's mother always said "No! Not until Dad's business gets a little better . . ."

Two years later, when Michelle was almost fourteen, the girl turned up in Michelle's 8th Grade science class.

Holly was nice enough, but no one seemed to like her. Maybe because she was older than the other kids. Maybe because she could answer all the teacher's questions and finish all the work before anyone else could. (But she rarely did.)

It could have been because she was more developed than any of the other girls. She had the figure of a grown woman.

Or maybe because she did whatever she wanted to, and didn't seem to care what anyone said or thought. Like when she would lollygag in the halls and slam the empty locker doors shut just to make noise. Or talk back to the teachers.

Then, of course, there were the rumors. She had stayed back twice because of truancy. She smoked, drank, and stayed out late. Supposedly, she already had sex, maybe many times. She was rumored to have brought a dildo to school with her once.

Word had it that she had oral sex with a boy in the bathroom.

But then, those were rumors.

There was that one day when Michelle was at her locker. Four of the popular girls gathered around Michelle and taunted her, making fun of the tight, greasy ponytail she usually wore. "Hey look, it's Willie Nelson!" the girls laughed.

"Stop!" said one of the girls. "Michelle doesn't look like Willie Nelson! He's way better looking!"

They all laughed again.

When Holly came around the corner, they all stopped laughing and hurried down the hall, whispering.

No one, especially the popular girls, had the nerve to make fun of Holly to her face. It was all done behind her back. And no one made fun of Michelle when she was with Holly. When Michelle was alone, they were merciless to her. Like when they put gum in her hair, threw rocks at her during recess, or threw her in a mud puddle. The other kids knew Holly would stand up to them if they made fun of either her or Michelle directly.

Michelle remembered her 8th Grade year. She was short, skinny, underdeveloped, and felt like a young, plucked, spring chicken.

Since her mother only let her shampoo every other night, every other day her hair was greasy. This didn't go unnoticed by the popular girls, who made fun of her. "Hey Michelle, can we go ice skating on your hair?" "Michelle, you're so ugly! Are you part Indian? Did you ever kiss a boy? Has anybody ever asked you out?" "Where did you get those clothes, Michelle, at the Salvation Army?"

How she would have loved to have had her hair done by a professional. But back then her family didn't have the money. Even if they did, her mother would still say: "Michelle, what's important is how you are on the inside, not the outside!"

Michelle shook her head sadly. It was like having an actress from a sappy, stupid TV show as a mother.

Once, in a moment of anger during an argument with her, Michelle called her mother a clueless, ditsy, white-bread suburban housewife. It made her mother cry.

Michelle had to use curlers, ribbons, bobby pins, and barrettes to manage her hair. And wear hand-me-down clothes. She always felt young and inferior.

The popular girls had such nice hair and clothes. That was what they lived for. You could never hope to be popular if you didn't have nice hair and clothes.

Holly's hair was always so clean, wavy, and full. But the popular girls wouldn't have noticed that, because Holly wore the wrong *clothes. Her clothes were either all black, too bright, or out of style. That didn't seem to bother Holly.*

She would think nothing of wearing white pants over bright bikini briefs, which she would often use as underwear. Or she would wear white pants over black panties. Or a ruffled Renaissance dress with fishnet stockings or black tights.

Sometimes she would wear a mini skirt with a garter belt showing. And the only time she might *wear a bra were the days they had gym.*

On the fourth day of school that year, Michelle saw the back of Holly's head with her long black hair. Holly was sitting alone in the cafeteria.

Micheile looked around. She couldn't decide where to sit. The jocks had their table. The popular girls had their table. Their game was to make sarcastic remarks to anyone who didn't hang around with them. Either that or look at each other and laugh at some silent, inside joke.

The straight-A students and nerds had their table. The musicians, artists, and actors had their table. And the druggies, criminals, and sluts had theirs. Michelle had no group to belong to. So, by default, Michelle sat down next to Holly. Holly's face was red and stained from crying. Tears welled in her eyes.

Holly looked at Michelle, and then turned away, picking at the institutional spaghetti that lay on her lunch tray. Finally, she forced a "Hi, Little Girl."

"What's the matter, Holly?" asked Michelle.

Holly never answered, but Michelle knew. Holly had realized that no one liked her. She also may have heard the whispering behind her back.

Michelle couldn't think of what to say, and, if she had, she probably couldn't have brought herself to say it. But it might have been something like: "I like you, Holly. I'll be your friend."

Michelle had known her best friend, Lauren, since Kindergarten. Since that time, she and Michelle were always in the same class. They were inseparable the whole time.

There were slumber parties, family exchange vacations, long telephone conversations, and many, many trips to the mall. But then something changed. Lauren began hanging around with the popular girls.

"I'll hang out with you after school," Lauren said to Michelle one day. "But in school I'll hang around with the girls who go to the yacht club. My dad hangs around with some of their dads . . ."

Michelle never really understood what that was all about. But it made her cry later, after she thought about it.

At first, Lauren stayed friends with Michelle. Then after a while the conversations grew strained and scarce. Then they would only say "Hi" in the halls. Then they would only nod to each other. Finally, there was no acknowledgement at all.

As Michelle would recall later, she may have first earned Holly's respect when she stuck up for Holly in class. The 8th Grade science teacher, Mr. Schuster, a burly man with a full beard and moustache, was yelling at Holly for not turning in her homework. One of the Straight-A+ students, a wiry boy with a crew cut and glasses blurted out: "She never does her homework! She should fail!"

Michelle looked at him. "Oh, shut up, Eraser Head! At least Holly has a life!"

Someone in the back whispered something about Holly to someone else. It wasn't nice.

Mr. Schuster looked at Michelle. "And what brought you into this conversation?"

"So she didn't do her homework. So deal with it."

"I'll deal with you right now. Michelle, you have detention!"

After class, Michelle put her head down on her locker and sobbed. She never got in trouble at school. If her mother ever found out, there would be hell to pay.

The next day Holly invited Michelle to sit with her at lunch.

One day Holly came in late to school. When she arrived, she had bleached-blonde hair, Michelle remembered. But her new locks didn't match her darker, auburn eyebrows.

It was right before gym class. Michelle hated gym because she wasn't athletic and often got hurt. When the other kids picked teams, there were heated arguments over who got stuck with Michelle. "It's your turn! We got stuck with her last time!"

The same kids were always captains.

That day Michelle saw one of the most traumatizing things she had ever experienced in her life.

"No one even cared about Holly." She remembered. "Holly couldn't even move. She was unconscious. At first I thought she was dead."

That day, Holly was wearing clothes that seemed several sizes too big for her. In fact, they were men's clothes. They included a shabby blue sweatshirt, blue jeans that didn't match, and sneakers twice the size of her feet.

Holly didn't mind gym because she was naturally athletic and could run much faster than most of the other girls.

When they played sideline soccer, Michelle and Holly figured out the system the gym teacher used to assign every player a number. They would line up accordingly. Michelle didn't feel as uncomfortable competing against Holly because Holly usually showed more mercy to Michelle than anyone else would have.

As the game progressed, the gym teacher threw the ball against the wall and yelled out: "Eight!" That was Holly and Michelle's number.

Holly ran from the line. So did Michelle.

"Holly was running funny." Michelle recalled. "I don't know whether her shoes were too big for her, or if she was running on her heels. All of a sudden, she fell down - face-first. The sound of her hitting the floor was awful! Like a redwood falling on a giant kettle drum! You could feel it! Everybody laughed! They all thought it was funny!

"Holly just lay there. She didn't get up or move. The gym teacher came over. She shook Holly and almost tried to turn her over, but didn't. Then she went to the office. The secretary came and knelt down next to Holly. Then Holly started to cry, and cry, but she didn't move a muscle. She cried really loud. She was crying so loud that the secretary looked around, nervously. Then another secretary came in and knelt beside Holly. Two more teachers from Special Ed came in. Holly kept crying and crying, but she still didn't move.

"The other kids were talking about how Holly was faking being hurt to waste time in gym. Some of the popular girls were laughing at Holly's clothes. Finally, Holly stopped crying."

"Holly is dead!" yelled a boy.

"No she isn't!" said another. "She's just sleeping!"

"I wanted to sit with Holly and hold her hand." recalled Michelle. "I wanted to tell her she'd be alright. But the teacher didn't let me. I guess after we all left the gym they took Holly away in an ambulance. She was out of school most of that week. When she got back, we never talked about it. Not about her getting hurt or the other kids laughing. Even during the day it happened, no one talked about her at all or asked if she was alright. I just can't believe, even to this day, how anybody could be that mean. I know they didn't like her, and at first they might've thought she was faking, but she was a human being, lying there hurt!"

Michelle remembered other things that happened at school. Like what she did to Ashley and Sarah, when she was their teacher. The things Holly did to her.

Late one night, Michelle snuck out of the house. Rick was asleep. He could sleep through anything – well, almost anything.

Michelle stepped out of her car with a bottle of wine in one hand, and a bouquet of geraniums, petunias, and marigolds in the other. After walking down a hill of manicured lawn, and stopping some fifty feet from a fountain, she saw a single headstone. 'HOLLY' was engraved on it.

She knelt down and gently laid the flowers beside it.

She took the cap off the bottle and held it up.

"Hi, Holly," she said, "do you remember this wine? We used to drink it a lot."

She took a swig from the bottle. Her head shook.

"It tastes just as bad. But it always got the job done. Right? We wanted to feel no pain. That's what happens when you drink this stuff."

Michelle drank. Then she drank some more.

"I miss you Holly. Really miss you. I have never met anyone quite like you. You were special. All my life, I just wanted a special friend. Someone I could really connect with, who understood me. I have that with Rick. But I always wanted a female friend too. Someone I could talk to. Who could relate to me as a female. *You* were that friend. I guess I'll never have another friend like you."

Michelle started to cry. ". . . oh, Holly! I'm so sorry! It wasn't right! It wasn't right! I'm so sorry! It wasn't supposed to happen! I'm so sorry, Holly!"

An hour went by before Michelle realized it. She lay down on the dewy grass and cried herself to sleep.

SIX

"I just wanted to remember something. I had a friend who lived here back in '82."

WHEN it poured rained for several days in a row, Michelle started to act stranger and stranger. Michelle couldn't sell ice cream, so she had a lot of time on her hands. And you know what the devil does with idle hands.

Michelle had something to do one night. She drove to the waterfront. Twilight Towers loomed up in the night with its curved arch balconies and gloomy green porch lights.

Michelle walked the length of the building.

Suddenly, she heard a girl scream.

Michelle turned and looked all around. No one was in sight.

Michelle looked up to the end unit on the fourth floor.

She heard that song in her mind, *Oysters In A Sandbox*.

'*. . . the days we had were ours/but we had too much fun/the chances that we took/were all 'cause we were young . . .*"

Michelle shivered. She looked away from the balcony. Then she looked back.

There was a girl staring down at her from the fourth floor. She had long black hair and stood in the glow of the green light. Part of a mask hid the left side of her face.

It couldn't be! No!

Michelle waved to Holly. Holly waved back.

"I'll be right up!" cried Michelle.

By the time she got to the front door, the buzzer was buzzing so she opened it and went in.

Michelle noticed the cheap wallpaper and carpets, similar to what was there before. The elevator still worked.

She pressed the Up button.

Once on the fourth floor, Michelle ran through the hall to the door and out onto the balcony. No one was there. Was she imagining things?

Michelle walked to the end unit. She looked at the railing. That was the last place she had seen Holly alive.

The curtains on the end unit were drawn.

She looked at the door to the condo. A tsunami of memories rushed at her.

The condo had belonged to an older man who let teenagers hang around whenever they wanted to. Rumor had it that he was connected to a wealthy family. But he had a bad reputation in town.

Michelle only met him once. It was a terrible day. But she couldn't think about that right now.

Her thoughts turned to when she and Holly were there alone one night.

Holly wore a blue bandana over her newly-colored auburn hair. She wore a black leotard and skin-tight blue jeans. Hanging from her lobes was a pair of tacky glass earrings your eccentric aunt might wear.

"This is good stuff!" said Holly. "Colombian!"

She held the burning joint in her hand while she tried to hold her breath to hold the hit she had just taken in. Her face was red and her eyes were glazed over; her pupils dilated.

"What's it like?" asked Michelle.

"Oh, you feel spacey, everything will seem funny, and you feel so relaxed . . ."

Michelle reached for it. Holly pulled it away.

"Not yet, Little Girl."

Little Girl. How that burned Michelle up inside.

"Please let me have some!"

Michelle knew the game Holly was playing. Holly could get her to do things by denying her at first. Or did she? Did she care enough about Michelle that she felt guilty about giving her drugs? Michelle never fully understood. Especially considering what happened.

"Shelly, you're just too young! Wait a few years!"

Michelle grabbed it and sucked in.

Fire burned her throat. Her eyes watered. She tried to hold it in, but coughed it out.

Holly laughed. "I told you!"

Then Michelle smoked some more. Then more. It had no effect on her. So she smoked more. She knew it wouldn't have any effect on her. So she smoked even more.

She could feel her heart beating. Heavy. Heavier. Even heavier.

Wow. Everything was moving in slow motion. She could hear the music from the stereo. Someone singing "Bought you flowers, candy too, I just want to make it up to you . . ."

The sound wrapped around her like a blanket.

There was a warm, pulsating sensation throughout her body. She could feel her heart pound.

Holly sat on the floor, talking on the phone to some guy. She would laugh every one in a while. But all of Holly's words had double meaning, and every word was really some kind of code or puzzle that Holly was putting out just for Michelle to solve. Or was she? Michelle was confused. Ordinary words were now confusing.

Did Holly really talk about the whipped cream? Apparently, her guy friend had stuck the nozzle to a can of whipped cream up her twat and sprayed the cream in there, then all over her body. Then he licked it off.

Hanging on the wall was an Indian mask with long, black horse hair. It was the most hideous face Michelle had ever seen.

"What's that?" asked Michelle, pointing to the mask.

Holly laughed. "I call her Judy."

The mask made Michelle uncomfortable. Was Michelle as ugly as the mask?

Holly showed Michelle a new pair of shoes she bought. They were pink pumps with red heart designs on the soles.

"Those are really nice, Holly."

"Thanks. I got them at a yard sale."

Michelle smiled, but she didn't know why. It was the sofa. It just looked funny, with all the stripes going up and down.

That night they made brownies, and ate ice cream, and everything seemed like a dream to Michelle. She wanted to wake up, but she couldn't. Then it became a nightmare.

31

The condo was a box, and she couldn't get out. Everything was sad; hopeless. How could she get home? Would she be able to find her way? What if she couldn't? What if the road had disappeared?

The last thing she remembered about that night was lying next to Holly as they watched TV. They watched Dallas. *Then* Falcon Crest.

How she wished her family had money like the people on those TV shows. Then she could afford new clothes, makeup, a stylist, and maybe even a trip to Disney World. Would her family ever go on a trip together again? Would she ever kiss a boy or even go on a date?

Holly played with Michelle's hair, stroking it, teasing it, and putting it into a ponytail. Michelle had started to wash her hair every day, in spite of her mother's orders.

"Shelly, you have to promise me something. See, you've got a future . . . I don't know if I do . . . I'll probably get pregnant before I'm 18; you have to promise me something, Shelly . . . you have to promise that you won't get too much like me . . . promise me . . . promise me . . ."

Her speech slurred, Holly fell asleep.

Michelle looked at Holly's sleeping face. The face of an angel. Her green eyes so innocent. Her face so pretty. She pretended to be so hip, cool, and happy. But Michelle knew Holly wasn't happy at all. It was all a front. What happened to make her like that?

They never discussed Holly's personal life. Not ever.

Finally, Michelle snuck out and went home late. Boy, was her mother mad!

Yes. That condo brought back memories. Michelle turned to leave and crashed into somebody.

"Michelle!"

"Megan!"

They stared at each other.

"Megan, what are you doing here?"

"I live on the second floor, Michelle."

"Oh."

"Michelle, are you okay? You keep twitching your wrist. Did you hurt it?"

Michelle looked at her wrist.

"No."

"Michelle, I just overheard a call on my police radio that someone was ringing doorbells here, and wandering around. Is that you?"

Michelle blushed. "I just wanted to remember something. I had a friend who lived here back in '82."

Megan nodded. "Well, it's really late. You must've scared someone by ringing their doorbell this late. You should go home and get some rest. They're sending an officer over. I'll just tell him it's alright."

Michelle nodded and started to walk away.

"I hear it's going to be eighty and sunny tomorrow!" said Megan. "Make sure you come by the station! And save a Starburst for me!"

Megan looked on as Michelle opened the door to go back inside. She remembered that incident as the forerunner to all the trouble.

SEVEN

"What was your worst trip?"

MEGAN was right. The next day was 82 and sunny.

Michelle sold ice cream the next day. But she didn't stop at the police station. Maybe she was too embarrassed to face Megan after what happened. Maybe she ran out of Starburst bars. Who knows?

Late the next night, Michelle and Rick had another conversation. Many secrets from the past came out. Some of them were quite disturbing.

It was probably after midnight that Michelle woke up. She couldn't get back to sleep, so she got out of bed. Rick was lying in hibernation. It would take an atomic blast to wake him up.

She wandered into the kitchen to get a glass of milk. When she turned on the light, she saw the magazine next to Rick's computer. She stared at it. It was an old wrestling magazine he had won on ebay.

But she had seen that magazine before. On the cover were two wrestlers, one with black hair, and the other with bleached blonde. The black-haired wrestler had the bleached blonde in some type of hold and the bleached blonde wrestler's mouth was opened, screaming in pain.

Where had she seen it before?

Her wrist started to twitch. She wasn't even aware of it.

She looked at the cover again, *The Wrestler*, June, 1982.

1982! June! It must have come out in May! May! That was the month that Holly . . . Holly . . .

Michelle had seen the magazine at the condo! The guy that lived there used to watch professional wrestling!

Oh, God, thought Michelle. It was starting to happen again. Holly. The balcony. Holly falling off. Her feet going over the railing . . . the scream. The crash below.

But she found out Holly was alive! Holly was going to be alright! Okay, she might be hurt, but she would be alright!

But Holly might tell! No! She hit her head! She had amnesia! How could she prove it? It was Holly's word against hers. Nobody could prove anything. Holly jumped anyway. She was on LSD and she thought she could fly.

But then Holly died. How terrible. Your best friend wasn't supposed to die. Okay, so she hit you sometimes. Everybody's friend hits them sometimes, right? And she got you in trouble. So what? Everybody gets in trouble sometimes. Well, almost everybody. Besides, you're sick of being good. Nobody respects you when you're good all the time. You have to be bad sometimes. Nobody even pays attention to you if you're good all the time, especially the guys.

And the drugs. Well, everybody tries them. They're okay once in a while. Yes, Holly takes way too much. Holly drinks way too much. But she'll get over it someday. She'll settle down. Everybody settles down. She'll get married and have a house and kids like everybody does. Like you will someday. Someday. Even your mother says that.

No more Holly. No more Lauren. It's just you against the popular girls. Boy, are they mean sometimes.

If they're so popular, why do they have to be so cruel? They have everything!

You can always go to The Caves. There will be other kids there. But it just wouldn't be the same without Holly. Plus, Holly could stop them when the boys got too rough . . .

You can't go back to that condo again. Not after what happened. Someone might recognize you. Someone might have seen you do it – no! You didn't do anything! She just fell, remember?

"What's going on?" Rick entered the room.

Michelle jumped. "Nothing."

He noticed her wrist twitching.

"How's your wrist?"

Michelle gave him a puzzled look. She felt it.

"Fine. It's okay. Why do you buy these things, anyway?" she pointed to the magazine.

"They remind me of a time in my life."

"Me too."

"What were you doing back then?" he pointed to the date on the magazine.

"A lot of stuff I shouldn't have. Sex. Drugs. Rock n' Roll. What were *you* doing back then?"

Rick sat down at the dining room table. Michelle sat across from him.

"I started smoking weed."

Michelle nodded.

"Once I tried it," he continued, "it was the best feeling in the world. I could hide from my problems. Any reason to smoke would do, like if a girl dumped me. Or if I met another girl.

"Then I wanted more excitement. So I tried mescaline, these tiny pills that were red, orange, blue, or purple. Actually, it wasn't real mescaline. Real mescaline comes from cacti. These were probably LSD, PCP, Speed, or rat poison."

"Rat poison?"

"Yeah. Small doses of rat poison will get you high. So drug dealers use it to dilute their product. They also use asbestos, since the grains are so fine. But mescaline . . . or whatever it was . . . me and my sister used to invite our friends over on Friday nights and have mescaline parties. They got really far out. The house would start spinning and people's heads would be shaped like mushrooms and everything. You'd laugh at everything. Then you'd turn on the TV and people would speed up and slow down when they talked and turn into gorillas. Ted Koppel used to look like he had half his head chopped off . . .

"Then we went outside. It was midnight. Nobody was on the streets. Then this fire engine came by. It totally freaked us out, all the noise, sirens, lights, going fast.

"I got us all paranoid by saying that if there were a fire, they'd blame it on us because we were the only ones out. We ran under the bleachers at the park, and then ran home. Then there was this plastic wrapping, caught in a tree, blowing in the wind. It scared the hell out of us! What a night!"

"What was your *best* trip?"

"Let's see . . . after we took blue one time, we skipped school and hung around downtown all day. It was winter and everything was beautiful. It was like a little European village . . . We were sitting in the food court and there was this picture of an ice cream cone on the wall. I couldn't stop laughing. Every time I looked away from the picture it would light up! It was the funniest thing I ever saw! I even said: "Stop lighting up over there!" My sister didn't even know what I was talking about! She said: "Nothing's lighting up over there!"

Rick sighed. "The only trouble was I punched my best friend in the face. I couldn't believe it. I just got paranoid! I thought he was trying to sneak off with my sister . . . He said: "If you can't handle drugs, then you shouldn't take them in the first place." Then he told me to: "Go find a park bench and mellow out!" I felt so bad for hitting him."

"What was your *worst* trip?"

"I'll never forget that one. I had bought some Panama Red and had been smoking it almost every day for a week. Then we met up with a guy and a girl near the beach who offered to sell us red mescaline. I was the only one who had any money, so I bought it. But I decided to save it for the next night, to take it before I went to see my cousin's high school musical. She was the star. *West Side Story*.

"Before we left for the show I smoked some pot, and then opened my container. The hit of mescaline was gone! I looked closely. It had turned to powder. I could see the red. So I wet my finger and dipped it in and put it to my tongue that way.

"I was laughing pretty hard the whole way over. Then it really started to affect me. I couldn't understand what people were saying. Everybody seemed to have some sort of weird foreign accent.

"During the play I was seeing skeletons coming at me. I thought everybody was talking about me. Then I kept thinking I was going to piss my pants. Then I thought I did. I hadn't. But I thought everybody was talking about that, too.

"So when intermission came, I ran out of the auditorium and told everybody I was sick. Actually, I was. It was the strongest buzz I had ever had, even compared to drinking a case of beer. I just wanted to come down. But then I found the secret to life and decided to change mine. Seeing my cousin as a star, a winner, and me a loser, put it all in place for. I knew I could be better than what I was. Drugs were destroying me. I would never do drugs like that again. I took mescaline one more time after that, but then that was it. I did keep smoking pot for a long time after that. I felt so inferior to everyone and everything. Mostly because I was skinny and had a club foot. Everybody made fun of my limp. I could understand the kids making fun of me; kids are cruel sometimes. But I would also hear adults. Talking about me behind my back. Laughing at me. Especially the gym teachers. People would ask my parents about it angrily, as if *I* wanted it or it was *their* fault I had it.

"What was *your* worst trip?" Rick asked Michelle.

He may as well have shot her. The condo. Holly. The vacuum cleaner. The baby in the window. *Oysters In A Sandbox*. That's the song that was playing. The balcony. The railing. The fall.

"I don't want to talk about it," she said.

"Oh, but I'm supposed to answer all *your* questions!"

"It was terrible. Just terrible."

"In what way?"

"It practically tore my head off. Headlights. A person in a mole's costume. That big, invisible machine. The guy on the street with the sunglasses was really a spy. The ape people. Eyes in the wall. Snakes. Peacock feathers flying. The Volkswagen bug. The dolls. The Indian mask. Any minute my heart was going to stop . . . the mirror . . . the window blowing open . . ."

"Where were you when you took it?"

"Twilight Towers."

"Oh, that place. Figures."

"Why does it figure?"

"Well, like we talked about, that building was known for drugs in the '80's."

Michelle nodded.

"I'll never forget what day I had that bad trip either," said Rick. "Saturday night, May 15, 1982."

Michelle's heart palpitated. "My friend Holly fell from Twilight Towers two days later!"

Rick's mouth fell open. His eyes opened wide.

"My grandmother told me about it!" he said. "Then I read about it in the paper! It was very mysterious. It really affected me emotionally. I felt so bad about it. It was almost like she was the sacrificial lamb. I had decided to change my life, and she was an example of what could happen to me if I didn't. I had a feeling it was drug-related."

Silence. They both stared into space.

"I've been thinking about that lately," Rick sighed. "There was something very strange about that incident. It just didn't make sense. There was hardly any coverage in the papers about it . . ."

"I know."

"What was the hardest drug you've ever done?"

Michelle thought about it. "I did cocaine a couple of times. Crack two or three. And we skin-popped heroin once – Holly and I. That's all. But I got really sick. Throwing up. Passed out. I couldn't move. I just lay by the window thinking I was going to die. I must've had a bad reaction. Thank God! I could've been a junkie!"

"I never tried coke, crack, or heroin."

"Don't!"

"Yes Ma'am! But I did try PCP – Angel Dust. Long before my worst trip."

Michelle shuddered. "What was that like?"

"Actually, I OD'd. I ended up in the fields thinking I was in Vietnam! I had no idea how to get out! Not that I had ever been to Vietnam!

"Finally, I crawled out of the woods and made it to the mall. I just lay on a bench, then on the floor. I kept thinking I was going to die. Then these two guys came up to me. They were the biggest druggies and dealers I ever knew. I was a big customer of theirs. They knew I was wasted and they asked me what I had taken. I told them it was Reds – a street name for PCP. They shook their heads and laughed. "You're one messed-up dude!" one of them said.

Rick shook his head. "Here were the two biggest druggies I ever knew, telling me *I* was messed up! They said they would never try PCP – Angel Dust – too dangerous. I was bad even by *druggie* standards!"

Michelle laughed.

"That PCP is totally unpredictable," Rick said. "It's a horse tranquilizer – that makes you hallucinate! People have ripped their own ears off and everything! You can't feel any pain! Some people never come down and get locked up in a mental hospital for the rest of their lives! And it's been known to make people violent – enough to kill someone!"

Michelle gasped. *She remembered something.* No! She couldn't think about that right now.

"Rick, you said you found the secret to life on that really bad trip that time, at your cousin's play. What is it?"

He thought for a while. "That everything's an illusion. We give our own meaning to things. That everybody has a style, or a con game to play and everything is about how something or someone is *packaged*. For example, I never thought that the so-called 'Good Kids', who were always ragging on other people about doing drugs, who were always wearing the 'right' clothes, or playing the 'right' sports, or in with the 'right' people used drugs. But they did! They were such hypocrites! That really bothered me. They condemned other people for what they were doing, but they did it too! And they never got in trouble for doing bad things because nobody wanted to believe they would do bad things!

"Like the theft ring. Four or five jocks were caught stealing, breaking into other kids' lockers. Yeah, they got in trouble, but not half as much as some 'bad' kid would have! Because the jocks were 'packaged' the right way. And when those other jocks broke into the school and trashed it after drinking one night, it made national news! All over the country! Broken windows, computers, bookshelves knocked down, everything! Something like fifty thousand dollars worth of damage! But did they go to jail? NO! Community service! Probation! Who went to jail? The 22-year-old who bought them the beer! He didn't do any damage! He wasn't a jock and he grew up in a foster home! They blamed it all on him – not the kids who drank the beer and did the damage!

"So I realized I had to look out for myself and do what I needed to do to get to where I wanted to go. I was planning on playing sports the next year and getting involved with the school's music and drama program. And so I did. I may have still smoked weed and drank occasionally, but now at least I was doing it with the 'right' people! I 'repackaged' myself!"

"Wow. I felt the same way too. But do you feel like you sold out?"

"No. Not really. I decided to play someone else's game and win – in my own way on my own terms."

Rick laughed. "So, when did you try coke?"

Michelle sighed. "It was at a party put on by the girls at the Loyola Marymount School in South Hanover. It was an all-girl Catholic school where Holly used to go. But they threw her out. They caught her drinking. That would've been funny to see - Holly wearing a catholic school uniform with a bottle of cheap wine!

"We were over at this girl's house, I think her name was Rachel, and there were two other girls. One was named Heather, and she had the prettiest, purest, blondest hair I had ever seen. I really loved playing with it and brushing it for her. How I wished I had hair like that. I forget the other girl's name, it might've been Kelly, but she was pretty too. Anyway, we all had ice cream and malts from this Frosty truck that was there. We were at a house on a hill where the yard sloped down to a river. There were like ten girls, and there didn't seem to be any adults. It was hot out.

"Holly had red hair that day, and she told me to come with her down the hill. Then she poured out this white stuff on a flat rock from an envelope, and she had a dollar bill rolled up into a straw. So she snorted some, then I did."

"How was it?"

"It was great! Probably the best high I've ever had! But I had a really bad headache after. I don't think Holly did it much. She was mostly a drinker. That stuff was too expensive anyway . . ."

"What about the other drugs?"

"At parties, mostly. I can't remember the details. Everybody could go away for spring break. I had to work two jobs just to pay for school. That really hurt. When all your friends can go away to places like Cancun and have nice clothes, new cars, and you can't. I was lucky to get used clothes from the church pantry that my grandmother used to work in. So I did drugs to escape the pain. I just can't believe how stupid I was!"

"We've all done stupid things. Especially as kids. I remember one night, drinking behind the pool hall; this kid showed us the gun he had just bought. I knew right then I was in the wrong place at the wrong time . . . all those kids are either dead now or in jail. One of them went to jail for murder."

They talked for another forty-five minutes before going to bed.

Michelle wondered how much longer she could keep her secret.

41

EIGHT

"I have to find Holly!"

MICHELLE'S nightmares were another warning sign. Unfortunately, Rick didn't know how to handle them either.

Michelle described one. It was quite vivid.

The girl with long, auburn hair, fair skin, and light freckles hugged Michelle. Michelle was crying and she had her arms around the girl's waist, with her fingers dangling near the girl's butt. She had a nice ass. Guys loved it. If only Michelle had an ass like that. Then all the guys would notice her. . .

"Oh, Shelly, I'm so sorry! It was an accident!" the older girl said into Michelle's ear. "You ran so fast and I was just putting up my arm to tease my hair!"

"I . . . ran . . . into . . . your . . . elbow . . ."

"I'm wicked sorry!"

"Please help me!" Michelle screamed.

"Okay. We'll get some ice. But you have to stop crying, Shelly! Your lip will be alright! It's not bleeding!"

"Thank you Holly. Thank you."

The older girl bent down and held Michelle by the wrist.

"Don't tell anybody!" she said. "If you get me in trouble I can't hang out with you!"

Michelle nodded. When she did, a tiny drop of blood fell from her lip and onto the railing of the porch balcony they were leaning on. The tiny drop, which went unnoticed except by a trained eye, stayed there for a long time.

The older girl cradled Michelle in her arms and carried her like a baby back inside.

The alarm clock rang. Michelle sat up in bed. Rick lay next to her, asleep. He could sleep through anything. Well, almost anything.

She felt her lip. It hurt. She had bitten it during her nightmare.

When she looked in the mirror, she noticed it was bleeding. That was when she remembered.

Holly put ice on her lip, hugged her, and played with her hair. Then Michelle took the ice away and noticed there was blood on it. Holly had lied to her.

Michelle looked in the mirror again. Suddenly, a strange fear came over her. The mirror image made two of her. She didn't want there to be two of her. That was when it happened. That man, at the condo, in 1982 . . . then Holly fell . . .

Michelle punched the mirror. It shattered glass all over the sink. Rick jumped awake.

"No!" screamed Michelle. "Holly! You fell from grace! I was bad to you! You were there for me! You slipped away!"

"Michelle! What's wrong?"

She had broken out in sweat.

Her pupils were dilated, her eyes had a glassy look, and she didn't make eye contact with Rick.

"You've been alone since '82!" she yelled. "You're among the stars!"

"You had a nightmare, Michelle. It's alright."

"Rick – Holly jumped! She thought she could fly after taking LSD – she jumped! It was terrible! I didn't remember it until now!"

She let out loud, anguished sobs.

"Michelle, I'm sorry! I thought it might be something like that! You must've blocked it out!"

He hugged her.

She screamed and cried.

The next day Michelle sold ice cream. She stopped at the school and sold Mr. Kinecki a Toasted Almond bar. Again, there was something very familiar about him. But Michelle couldn't figure it out. That bothered her.

When Mr. Kinecki would leave for the day, the kids on the track field above where he parked his car would gather at the fence and all yell out in unison: "GOODNIGHT, MOE!"

Then Ashley and Sarah bought their ice cream. They acted like it never happened. Michelle couldn't look them in the eyes that day.

Riding down the tree-lined street near the school, she saw one of her regular customers, a boy named Jason. He was a large, overweight boy whose hair and clothes were usually unkempt.

Michelle rang her bell as she passed him.

"Hi, Jason!"

He looked at her. His eyes were full of tears.

"Hi, Ice Cream Girl. I don't have no money today."

"You mean you don't have *any* money today. I used to be an English teacher, remember?"

She felt sorry for him. He always walked home alone. Apparently, he had no friends.

As Michelle rode by the entrance to the woods, she saw a group of teenage boys with long hair and scruffy clothes. Two of them had skateboards.

"Hey, Ice Cream Girl!" one of them yelled. "Give us some free ice cream!"

She smiled and kept riding.

Later that day, Michelle stopped at the police station. Megan came out, her long, wavy hair blowing in the wind. Usually she tied it in a bun.

She wasn't wearing a uniform, and she wore her badge on a necklace.

"So, is this the new look?" asked Michelle.

Megan smiled and nodded. "Yeah. Normal clothes. Hair down. The usual, please. We missed you yesterday! We kept wondering when the ice cream girl was going to come!"

Michelle frowned and reached into the freezer. She handed Megan the Starburst and took the money.

"Michelle, is everything alright?"

Michelle stared into space and had a glassy look to her eyes.

"Michelle?"

"*All those dreams you had, when your eyes were barely*

green . . ." Michelle sang.

"What?"

Michelle snapped out of it. "I have to find Holly!"

She rode away.

As Megan licked her ice pop, she wondered who Holly was. Again, it gave her a sense of foreboding.

Megan finished her ice pop and went back inside. She and her partner, Sergeant Victor Gutierrez interviewed an elderly woman whose purse was stolen.

Megan leaned back in her office chair. Her handcuffs, snapped around one of her belt loops, dug into her back. Her service revolver tapped against her hip.

"Mrs. Miller," she said, "you have to try to remember if the man who stole your purse was Black or Puerto Rican – it makes a big difference! We have to find the right guy!"

Victor smiled. He was short and heavy-set, with a close crew cut and a pleasant smile.

"He was a big man, almost seven feet tall with a chest the size of a truck!" said the woman. She used her hands to show how big the man was.

Victor laughed.

"Okay," said Megan, "what kind of clothes was he wearing?"

The woman's face scrunched up. "Nice clothes."

Megan rolled her eyes. "What *color* were they?"

"He had on a bright blue jacket with gold buttons and bright red pants and he had a hat on . . ."

"What did his hat look like?" asked Megan.

"It was orange, with a red feather in it . . . and he had on a mask . . . ."

Victor threw his pen on the desk.

"Wait a minute!" he said. "How do you know he was black or Hispanic if he was wearing a mask?"

Mrs. Miller shrunk in her chair. "Ah, where's the powder room?"

Megan pointed to the hall. The elderly woman got up and left.

"Let's put out an A.P.B.," said Victor, "for a male who's built like Hulk Hogan, and dresses like Bozo the Clown."

Megan laughed.

Turning to her computer, and surfing the web, she went back to the website of the investigative hypnotist, Dunn. She did it often.

TEN

"You better not tell anybody what we do. If you do, I can't hang out with you anymore!"

RICK got used to Michelle's increasingly bizarre behavior. The waking up from the nightmares. The twitching of her wrist. The muttering of the lyrics from *Oysters In A Sandbox*. The strange fascination for young girls who had Holly's basic features. And the sneaking out late at night.

"It's just a phase I'm going through," Michelle said once. "I'll get over it. Thank you for being so patient with me."

Then the behavior got more and more bizarre.

When he first saw them, Rick thought they were only temporary tattoos. Later, it turned out they were permanent.

One of them was a dagger. It appeared on Michelle's forehead one day.

The other was a teardrop, under Michelle's left eye. Apparently, Rick didn't know what they stood for.

In restless walks Michelle prowled the night. She said it was because she couldn't sleep. If she slept, she would have nightmares.

On one of those late night trips, Michelle snuck into the school.

It hadn't changed much from when she taught there, or from when she was a student there herself. The first place she went was the gym.

That wooden floor was hard. One day, when they were playing Tag in gym, Michelle ran to tag Holly. Holly put up her hand and knocked Michelle off balance. Her knees hit the floor. She screamed and cried and the school nurse carried her out. Boy, did it hurt!

Michelle left the gym.

As she went by the stairway, she saw the banister post. It was metal and had a triangular point.

One day when Michelle was running to recess in the crowded hall, someone bumped into her and her forearm sliced on the metal point. It cut a deep gouge in Michelle's forearm. And she still had the trace of the scar, over twenty years later.

Michelle went out the door.

Once outside, something made Michelle go around to the back of the school. There, next to the wall, was a cement walkway. That was where the students lined up after recess before they went back inside. The same place Michelle and Holly had to line up. There was always pushing, shoving, jostling, and cutting the line. Some of it was good-natured, some of it wasn't. Once in a while, someone got hurt.

It was a warm, spring day and the kids were lining up. Holly sauntered over to the area as usual. Michelle didn't see Holly out at recess that day. Holly got sent to the office by Mr. Schuster for talking back to him again. She was late for lunch, and lazily ate her lunch once she got to the cafeteria. So by the time she got outside, there were only a few minutes left of recess.

Michelle walked slowly over to the line. She never understood why everybody wanted to be first in line for everything, especially when going back into school on such a warm, beautiful day.

Michelle was near the end. Holly came up to her.

"Hey! Little Girl!" said Holly. "You cut me!"

"No I didn't!"

"Yes you did!"

Holly grabbed Michelle's wrist with both her hands. She used one hand to hold Michelle's arm and the other to twist Michelle's wrist. Pain shot into Michelle like a needle.

"Cut it out!" said Michelle. She held back tears.

Holly put her lips up to Michelle's ear and whispered: "You better not tell anybody what we do. If you do, I can't hang out with you anymore!"

Michelle burst into tears.

"Why are you two holding hands?" asked a boy with glasses.

"SHE TWISTED MY WRIST!" screamed Michelle.

All of the popular girls, at the front of the line, laughed.

47

"Shut up!" screamed Michelle. "I hate all of you! You think you're so goddamned great but you're nothing! You'll never be anything but mindless robots all your lives! You don't accept anybody who's different from you because you're afraid you'll stand out! You're just a bunch of losers! All of you! And you make me sick!"

Michelle didn't care what she said. Words were just coming out of her mouth.

The popular girls laughed louder.

Holly hugged her. Michelle pushed her away. Holly hugged her again.

Michelle noticed that Holly was growing love handles above her hips. She jiggled them to insult her.

"I'm sorry Shelly," whispered Holly. "I didn't know you were going to cry."

Michelle put her arms around Holly and buried her face in Holly's chest. Holly had boobs. Michelle did not. She wished she had boobs like Holly.

Michelle noticed her former best friend Lauren staring at her, with a look of pity. She was standing with the popular girls. How she hated for Lauren to feel sorry for her.

"DON'T LOOK AT ME!" screamed Michelle. "Lauren, don't look at me when I'm crying!"

The popular girls laughed even louder.

Holly stroked Michelle's hair.

"It's alright," she said, rubbing her back. "Don't even look at them."

Her wrist hurt her so much that she went to see the school nurse. But the nurse wasn't there.

The first time Michelle wore a bra to school the popular girls whispered to each other and looked at Michelle, laughing.

That day at lunch, all the popular girls were sitting at a table with Lauren. Lauren didn't look happy.

Laughing, they invited Michelle to sit with them. Joy almost burst within her, and she couldn't help smiling. Imagine that, being invited to sit with the popular girls!

One of them asked Michelle: "Hey Michelle, if you had no hands, would you wear gloves?"

"What?"

"Guys, that's really mean . . ." Lauren had tried to say.

"If you had no hands, would you wear gloves?"

"What do you mean?"

"Just answer the question. Michelle, if you had no hands, WOULD YOU WEAR GLOVES?"

"No."

"Then why are you wearing a bra?"

They all burst out laughing. Even Lauren rolled her eyes and smiled.

"I'm sorry, Michelle," said one of the popular girls. "Actually, you know, you're pretty. Pretty ugly!"

"Michelle, you have lips like petals," said another girl. "Bicycle pedals!"

They all laughed again.

Michelle got back in her car. She drove by the wooded area near the school and stopped.

One day, she and Holly were smoking cigarettes in the woods before school started.

There was another girl with them, an older girl who went to the high school. Michelle never knew her name and really didn't care anyway. The girl wore skin-tight jeans, a red blouse with cleavage down to here, and all the jewelry and makeup you could ever need or want.

Holly spent more time talking to the other girl and barely paid any attention to Michelle. They talked about drugs, and bands, and sex, and drinking.

"I once drank a whole pint of Southern Comfort in one swig!" said the high school girl.

"Yeah, right," said Michelle, under her breath.

"What?" said Holly.

"Nothing."

"Little Girl, don't you have to go to school?"

Michelle blew smoke at Holly's face. Holly slapped her.

Michelle felt a tear roll down her cheek.

"Oh, look, she's going to cry!" laughed the high school girl.

They both pointed at Michelle and laughed.

Something came over Michelle. It was like someone had taken over her body and she had no control over it. She ran at Holly, swinging her arms.

Holly didn't even stop laughing as she grabbed Michelle's wrists, twisted them, and threw her on the ground. Her hands and knees were scraped.

Michelle limped and staggered towards the school. Near the front door was Lauren. Lauren gave her that pity look again, but then turned away. Michelle screamed and sobbed, trying to open the door. She could barely get it open. Nobody even helped her.

She went down the hall and sat on the nurse's bench.

Holly didn't mean it. She just wanted to impress that older girl. She and Holly would still be friends.

Later that day, Holly came up to Michelle, crying.

"Shelly, I'm so sorry!" She wiped the tears from her face. "Sometimes when I get high I get paranoid, and think people are out to get me! Even you! Please forgive me! It will never happen again, I swear!"

And it never did.

There was so much pain. Running into Holly's elbow. Holly tripping her in gym. Twisting and squeezing her wrists and hands that day.

Michelle twitched her wrist.

Then there were the accidents. Like when they were running to see who could get to the wooden fence at the park first, and Michelle was actually ahead of Holly! She was going to beat Holly at something, finally! She was so busy watching Holly that she ran into the fence post. Boy, did that hurt! Her head, her chest, her arm, her knee, and her foot. Holly helped her home.

"Holly, maybe you should tone it down just a little . . . maybe you're taking too many drugs . . ."

Wow. She had never said anything like that to Holly before. She felt like a mother talking to a child.

Holly nodded and hugged Michelle.

"That girl today, she's not my friend. She just sold me some weed. Only you are. You're my only friend. I love you. Please say you'll always be my friend! Please say you'll always be my friend!"

Holly sobbed even more. Michelle had never seen her in such a state.

Then Holly actually got down on her knees and hugged Michelle, burying her tear-soaked face in Michelle's white t-shirt.

Michelle played with Holly's hair and rubbed Holly's face, wiping away the tears.

"I will Holly. I will. I promise."

Not long after that, Michelle's mother forbade Michelle to hang out with Holly. A bottle of wine had slipped out of Holly's coat when she came to Michelle's house one night. It was that cheap stuff that always gave you a headache after you drank it.

That only made Michelle want to hang out with her more. So they snuck around. Her mother may have loved her, but Michelle had a right to choose her own friends. Besides, her younger sister, Maureen, had some real losers as friends. She was allowed to hang around with them. So Michelle could hang around with whomever she wanted to.

One day at the park, Holly and Michelle got high. No. Holly never got high. *Michelle got high. Holly always got* wasted.

Anyway, they got ice cream from the ice cream truck.

"I want to drive an ice cream truck someday!" Holly had said. "And make kids happy!"

Michelle remembered that as an insight into Holly's psyche. If Holly couldn't be happy herself, she could make other people happy instead.

As Michelle drove around, she remembered the incident that made her decide to leave teaching.

It happened during the '80's dance. The '80's dance. What were they thinking?! The PTO had decided to have an '80's dance to raise money.

Mr. Kinecki had roped Michelle into chaperoning.

They turned the gym into a carnival of '80's memorabilia. There were posters from the movies E.T., Tootsie, Rocky III, An Officer And A Gentleman, and Porky's. Michelle remembered seeing Porky's. She hated it. A fantasy for thirteen-year-old boys.

Hundreds of Rubik's Cubes hung from the ceiling.

The boys all crowded around arcade video games. There was *Space Invaders, Frogger, Pac Man, Asteroids, Galaxian,* and *Berzerk.* Then there was a racing car driver's game where you sat down and steered, and a submarine game where you stood and looked through a periscope as you shot torpedoes at passing battleships, PT Boats, and sea mines, while trying to avoid depth charges.

The DJ played J. Geils' "Centerfold", then Rick Springfield's "Jesse's Girl." Then it was Quarterflash's "Harden My Heart". Then Van Halen's "Jump" and "Dance the Night Away."

The dance floor was crowded as the students grooved to the beat. In no time, the gym was filled, almost to capacity.

The DJ announced: "The '80's were an ephemeral, decadent time of fun and excitement . . ."

The next song touched a nerve in Michelle. Her wrist began to twitch. She probably wasn't conscious of it.

The song was from 1982. The DJ played "Only Time Will Tell" by Asia.

Michelle heard that song on the radio constantly that summer, '82. Every time she heard it, she thought of how Holly had left her. She thought of all the fun they planned to have that summer; the summer that never came.

"Michelle!" It was Mr. Kinecki. "How's everything going?"

"Fine!" she yelled over the noise. "The kids seem to be having a good time!"

There was something so strangely familiar about him. But Michelle could not figure it out.

Holly. Wouldn't she get a kick out of this '80's dance? Wasn't Holly caught up in the partying '80's?

Michelle almost bumped into a Rubik's Cube, hanging from the ceiling. Then she had a flashback -- there was one in the condo that day!

She began to sweat. She could hear sounds coming from the colors. They were like a heavenly choir buried in special effects.

She walked to the front door, wiping her face, to see how the girls were doing selling tickets. Any more people, they might have to have them wait in line. The gym only had so much capacity . . . what was it again? A thousand? More?

Ashley and Sarah were standing in the hall by the door, manning the ticket table.

The song "Open Arms" by Journey was playing. Why all these songs from 1982? Was it 1982?

Then the D.J. played another song, not from '82, "Major Tom (Coming Home)." Michelle relaxed and her wrist stopped twitching. Soon another song blared from the speakers. It hit her like a train. She began to tremble, and her wrist began to twitch.

"There once was a time when I was bad to you . . ."

Suddenly, a series of flashbacks hit Michelle's mind one after the other: Holly standing on the balcony railing -- a baby in a window watching -- the sound of a vacuum cleaner -- wind blowing a window open -- a Rubik's Cube -- a tiled floor -- a man sitting next to her -- someone playing a guitar -- a wrestling magazine cover -- a scream -- a crash -- music playing "Oysters in a sandbox, that is what we are . . ."

Michelle almost fainted.

"Mrs. M., are you alright?" asked a boy.

Everything was coming at her at once. People. Yelling kids. Flashing lights. Loud music. That song. That song!

Michelle stepped outside. The air was much cooler.

There were cars from the '80's in the parking lot. There was a Chevy Nova, a Camaro, a Ford Pinto, and a Corvette. Apparently, some of the parents had brought their '80's cars out to create even more of an effect.

Michelle had to get away from that song.

When the song was over, Michelle went back in.

Holly – wait! It was Ashley, not Holly – she and Sarah were taking turns using a digital camera. They were practicing candid shots for the yearbook.

"Ashley! You said I could use it now!" Sarah reached for the camera. Ashley held it up. Sarah tried to grab it again. Ashley grabbed Sarah's hands. Then Ashley put both of her hands on Sarah's wrist and twisted it.

"Ow!" Sarah sank to her knees.

A pain shot up Michelle's arm.

"HEY! STOP IT!" screamed Michelle. She ran over and pushed Ashley against the wall. Ashley hit her head.

"Mrs. M.!" Ashley was shocked and horrified.

"Ashley! I'm sorry! Are you alright?! I just thought you were going to hurt her!"

Ashley was speechless and shaking. Sarah stood up. She had tears in her eyes.

"It's okay, Mrs. M. She was just kidding around. I'm alright."

But Ashley had twisted her wrist. *Why her* wrist? *Why?*

She had no right to do that to Ashley. Michelle knew that. But why the wrist? She felt her own wrist and rubbed it.

Nobody reported it. Not either of the girls or Michelle. But Michelle knew she couldn't teach anymore. So she quit at the end of that year.

When she told Rick about it, he was supportive.

"So you lost it for a second," he said. "Everybody flips out once in a while. Especially at such a high-stress job as teaching. That's a job I could never do. I just don't have the patience."

"I want to sell ice cream and make kids happy."

"If that's what you want to do, then go for it!"

"It'll be good exercise so my butt won't get too big!"

"You don't even have a butt!"

"Exactly!"

They both laughed.

Later, Michelle did something else. It shocked a lot of people.

ELEVEN

"These woods are dangerous!"

NO one, not even Michelle, knew the exact moment she went over the edge. Maybe there wasn't one. Maybe it was just a cumulative effect from everything that was going on.

After everything happened, many people had their own take on Michelle's strange behavior. Two of them were Ashley and Sarah. They told Megan about the incident where Michelle pushed Ashley into a wall. But they begged her to keep it a secret.

"I was really shaken up by it," said Ashley, "but I never told anybody because Mrs. M. is the most awesome teacher! And she gives us free ice cream sometimes!"

Sarah nodded in agreement.

"It was my fault!" said Ashley. "She really thought I was going to hurt Sarah!"

Sarah shuddered. "But she called Ashley *Holly*!"

"And one time when we were buying ice cream from her," said Ashley, "she had this really strange, spaced-out look in her eyes. Like she was on drugs or something! She said to me: 'Holly please take good care of Sarah and don't hurt her. You promised. I'm sorry I couldn't save you, like you saved me!'"

"Then she snapped out of it," said Sarah, "and acted like nothing happened. It was really weird."

Late at night, Michelle drove by Twilight Towers and looked up to the fourth floor. The first condo was the only one that had the lights on. The others just had those green porch lights. Michelle thought they looked eerie and creepy.

Maybe Holly was there, right now. Holly practically lived there at this point. Michelle never really knew if Holly was having an affair with the guy who lived there . . .

Up ahead, walking by the railing near the seawall, in the moonlight, Michelle saw her; a girl with black feathered hair.

Michelle pulled over and got out.

"Holly!" cried Michelle.

The girl didn't turn around.

"Holly, wait!"

The girl turned around, but then turned back and kept walking, faster.

Michelle caught up to her.

"Were you talking to me?" asked the girl.

"Holly! How are you? You gave us quite a scare! But you're all right now?"

"Ah, I'm not Holly!"

"Holly, it's alright! I'm really sorry! I shouldn't have done that! But you're okay!"

"Ah, I think you've got me mixed up with someone else." The girl spoke with a whiny, teenage voice. She tried to get past. Michelle grabbed her by the arms.

"Holly, tell me you forgive me! I know you got hurt! But please forgive me! We need each other, please, Holly!"

The girl started to cry. "Please let go of me! You're hurting me! I'm not who you think I am!"

A dog barked. Michelle turned to see a man walking the dog, smoking a cigarette.

The girl suddenly broke away from Michelle and ran to him. The man was so surprised, he jumped back.

"Please help me!" cried the girl. "She's crazy! She thinks I'm someone else! She keeps talking crazy stuff!"

The dog started to snarl and bark at Michelle. The girl ran behind the man, using his body as a shield.

"Is this a joke?" asked the man. But when he saw that the girl was crying, he reached for his cell phone.

"It's alright," said Michelle. "I'll leave. But I'm always here for you, Holly. Whenever you want to talk. Remember, I care about you. I'll always be your friend, no matter what, like I promised that day."

She got back in the car and drove away.

The police came and took statements. Megan happened to see the police reports at the station the next day. Right away, she knew it was Michelle. She recognized the name 'Holly.'

Megan planned on having a talk with Michelle about that incident when Michelle came by to sell ice cream. But Michelle never showed up.

Then something else happened.

That night, Michelle drove some more. And more. Then she stopped at a park that had many weeping willow trees. A brook ran through it.

The morning mist was coming over the water, onto the land. The full moon was shining its light through the trees and on the water. It was like a dream, a fantasy.

Michelle remembered more and more about Holly. Sometimes, when they were together, Holly would answer questions for her, like when she was arguing with her mother or getting in trouble at school.

"Why are you late for class?" yelled the science teacher.

"Because I'm not on time," said Holly.

"Because I'm not on time," said Michelle.

When Michelle was alone, she would talk the way Holly talked. And she would act the way Holly acted. But when it was her and Holly, she was just Michelle. When Holly wasn't with Michelle, was she still Holly?

The funeral. Michelle went to the wake.

Her mother hugged her before she went out the door.

"I'm so sorry about your friend, honey," she said. "Do they know how she fell?"

"No, Mom."

"Hey, why don't you start hanging around with Lauren again?"

LAUREN! 'Because I'm not good enough for Lauren.' Michelle thought to herself. LAUREN! How could she even say that name? Where was Lauren now, when Michelle needed her?

She went to the funeral home and looked in the room. The casket was opened, surrounded by flowers. They were big, bright, beautiful flowers. Petunias, geraniums, and many, many, others. Holly would've loved them. She had some in her hands, which crossed over her chest. Holly wore a pink dress with white lace.

Candles flickered on either side of the casket. Soft organ music filled the room.

She never saw Holly's face. But she could see the black hair. It was Holly's hair all right, stiff and matted down with hairspray.

Michelle realized that Holly's pretty green eyes would never see again. "And all those dreams you had/when your eyes were barely green . . ."

Holly's eyes had that shine about them; always dancing around. If only she had pretty eyes like Holly's. Hers were just plain brown.

Michelle could not bring herself to go in the room. It was just too sad.

Holly's mother, father, and younger sister were standing by the casket looking pale, crying.

They seemed like nice people. Her father was just too tired and zapped out to try to control a wild teenage daughter anymore.

Holly's mother seemed like a typical suburban house mom. This had to be the worst day of her life.

They even lived in a typical suburban house on a typical suburban street – Cherry Hill Road.

Holly's sister, who Michelle had never spoken to, seemed devastated. She was sobbing.

Holly said that her sister hung around with some real losers.

Nowadays they make such a big deal of getting grief counselors when a kid dies. There were no grief counselors for me, Michelle thought. People didn't do things like that back then. Everybody went about their business. It was like Holly never existed. Did she?

Was it Michelle's imagination, or did Lauren actually tell her how sorry she was? Maybe it was just wishful thinking.

So Michelle remembered Holly. And Holly would some day remember Michelle.

Michelle and Holly. Holly and Michelle. Holly, meet Michelle. Michelle, meet Holly. Could it be that . . . no! They were not the same person! Were they? No. Impossible.

After selling ice cream the next day, and as it became dark, Michelle stopped the bike and wandered into the woods on foot. She had to find Holly.

But she got lost.

When she got to The Caves, she remembered the night Holly brought her there.

That night was the first time Michelle went there. It was a warm spring night during April vacation.

It was a fantasy night. It was Michelle's first kiss. Well, her first real kiss anyway.

His name was Brian, and that's all she really knew about him. He was skinny, like her, with long, scraggly brown hair, and he wore a green cotton t-shirt with a pocket in the front just big enough for a pack of cigarettes. They were Marlboro, and the red and white logo stuck out from his pocket.

He wore tight blue jeans and a studded belt. When it got colder that night, he put on his leather jacket.

His work boots were dirty and scuffed.

Oh, what a stud!

A bunch of kids were gathered by the fire, drinking beer. There were coolers strewn about, and one kid was sitting on one.

When they came up to the gathering, Michelle could smell the pot smoke. Loud rock music was playing.

"Hey, Holly!" A kid with long blonde hair and a rugged face said, passing her a beer.

"This is my friend, Michelle. I call her Shelly. Hey Shelly, this is Brian!"

Holly grabbed him by the arm as he walked past. He was so shy he could barely look at Michelle. She smiled at him. He smiled back.

They sat together and he lit a joint. She shared it, and they made small talk. He was from out of town, staying with his grandmother during April vacation. He lived one town over.

He actually liked the same music she did. They found that out when the song "Party On The Hill" came on the radio, followed by "It's Friday Night", "4th of July" and "Deirdre."

Soon they were holding hands. Then he had his arm around her. After awhile he lifted her chin up gently and put his lips to hers. She had her eyes open but closed them when she saw his eyes closed. Then they were sharing their tongues. Michelle had never French kissed before. She felt an overwhelming feeling of joy and love that she could never put into words.

Holly was yelling, standing near the edge of the cliff, showing off for some boys.

The rest of the night became somewhat of a blur, with all the pot and beer Michelle had taken. She might have seen Holly go into the woods with Brian, but he was back with her later. Then they talked about getting together sometime, but never did.

She saw him at the mall near Christmas time that year, and they were friendly, but then nothing much happened after that.

As it got later, the crowd thinned out. There was just Holly, Michelle, and the rough-looking blonde kid who had put on a red bandana. He poked at the fire with a stick to keep the embers going.

"Oh, Man, I'm wasted!" he yelled.

Michelle was fascinated by him, so she came closer to talk. She wasn't attracted to him, but wanted to find out more about him in her stoned, drunken stupor.

"That's right!" slurred Michelle. "Keep that fire going!"

"You're kind of young to be coming here," he said to her.

"Naw!"

Somehow, some way, he just started kissing her about the face. It reminded Michelle of something bad that happened to her once.

Then he put his hands up her shirt.

"Ah, I've got to go . . ." she said, looking around for Holly.

Holly was slumped against a rock, smoking a cigarette.

". . . leave her alone . . . she's just a kid . . ."

Holly could barely talk, her speech was so slurred.

Then he moved his hands to her hips.

"Stop!" said Michelle. "I don't even know you!"

Holly was on her feet now. She pushed the kid away and pulled Michelle closer.

"Fuck off!" said Holly. "She's just a little girl!"

That may have been the only time Michelle didn't mind Holly calling her that.

How Michelle got home that night, she didn't remember. But she did remember a conversation they had. It went something like this:

". . . but Shelly, you have to do it sometime . . ."

"I will, when I'm sixteen. Maybe eighteen. And I want it to be with the right boy!"

It turned out to be anything but what she expected.

Rick found the ice cream bike near the entrance to the woods. There was no sign of Michelle.

Since she didn't come home that night, he drove around looking for her. That's when he saw the bike.

He called the police. One of the officers who came was Megan.

"These woods are dangerous!" he told her. "All those teenagers and homeless people hang around at The Caves! *People have been killed there!*"

The last sentence hit Megan close to home. She looked away.

". . . back in the '80's there was a paramilitary gang of Vietnam vets in these woods!" Rick ranted. "They used to rob people and hunt wild animals! Are they still here?"

Megan shook her head. "I heard about that. I think the National Guard rounded them up in the early '90's . . ."

"Then I wonder what happened!"

"Where's her money box?" asked Megan.

Sure enough, it was gone.

"Those teenage punks must've robbed her!" yelled Rick. "They must've taken her in the woods . . ."

What a manhunt. Dogs. The state police arrived. Helicopters with search lights flew overhead. The Sheriff's SWAT team rolled in. Three fire engines showed up. The firemen set up floodlights. Volunteers from the neighborhood helped search.

But they never found Michelle.

TWELVE

"I don't know what to think. This is one of the strangest cases I've ever seen."

THE next day brought rain and thunderstorms. Clouds so dark it seemed like night. Blinding rain. Thunder that sounded like two high speed trains colliding. Lightning like a laser beam. Winds that bent tall pine trees in half.

When night fell it continued. The streets of the town turned bare.

The lightning flashes brought daylight in the middle of the night.

The next morning, a group of teenage boys found the lifeless body of a woman hanging in a tree with a hangman's noose. She had long brown hair.

Megan and a bunch of other officers came. The woman hanging was homeless; she wasn't Michelle.

A young woman wandered into the police station shortly after midnight. Soaking wet, her torn white clothes were covered with mud. Her hair went in every direction. Her face was pale.

She shivered and she twitched her wrist.

When the officer working the desk saw her, he jumped.

"I need to talk to Detective Megan Downs," said the woman.

"She's not on duty now. Hey! Aren't you . . ."

"Can you call her please; it's a matter of life or death."

Megan came in the back door. After putting on her badge necklace, she went to the lobby.

There was the woman; pale, soaked, and shaking.

"Michelle! My God! What happened to you?"

62

Michelle looked into Megan's big, brown, understanding eyes and burst into tears.

Megan took her to a back conference room. She wrapped a blanket around Michelle and gave her a cup of coffee.

"Michelle, do you need to go to the hospital?"

"No."

"Did someone attack you? What happened?"

"I was just wandering around in the woods and got lost."

"Didn't you see the search parties looking for you?"

"Megan, I don't remember much about anything!"

"I don't understand. Did you hit your head, Michelle?"

"No. Megan, I've got to tell you something. *I murdered my best friend over twenty years ago!*"

Megan's heart palpitated.

Michelle put her head down and let out loud, anguished sobs.

Megan sat next to her and put her hand on Michelle's shoulder.

"Are you sure?"

Michelle nodded. "Everybody thought she fell off the balcony. We were tripping on LSD. If I got caught I was going to say she jumped off thinking she could fly. That's what's happened to other people who took it!"

"Michelle, before you say any more, I have to tell you that you have the right to remain silent . . ."

Michelle wrote furiously on the yellow legal pad Megan gave her. Through the black and white video monitor, Megan and her partner Sergeant Victor Gutierrez looked on.

"She's really a mess," said Victor. "Look at how she keeps twitching her wrist. She's definitely not playing with a full deck."

Michelle finished writing. She sat up straight in her chair.

The two detectives went in and sat across from her.

Victor grabbed the legal pad and began to read.

"Michelle," said Megan, "two nights ago, did you stop your car and shake up a teenage girl, calling her *Holly*?"

Michelle sobbed. "I don't know! The last few days were such a blur! I don't even know, Megan!"

"Michelle, are you on any kind of medication?" asked Victor.

"No!"

"Use any drugs?" asked Megan.

"Not since I was in college!" She held up her forearm. "You can check my blood!"

Megan noticed the scar. She pointed to it. "How did you get that?"

"Someone pushed me into a banister post when I was in 8th Grade."

Victor showed Megan something Michelle had written on the pad:

HOLLY KEPT CALLING ME LITTLE GIRL. I TOLD HER NOT TO. SHE GOT UP ON THE BALCONY RAILING AND I PUSHED HER OFF.

Megan and Victor left the room.

"I don't know," said Victor, "this is shaky. They can't make her testify against herself. Wow, 1982. Both of us were little kids back then."

"I was only two!"

"You'll have to do some research, Megan."

"Me? Thanks a lot Victor!"

"She came to *you*. She trusts *you*. She's your ice cream girl! Go dig up the police reports from twenty years ago. We must still have them. Look up the old articles in the newspapers. Talk to Lieutenant Dodge; he was a rookie back then. You know *him*. He remembers *everything*."

Megan looked into the incident at Twilight Towers. *What she found out scared the hell out of her.*

It wasn't exactly what Megan found out that scared her, but what she didn't find out. Yes, there was an incident at Twilight Towers, and yes, a girl named Holly had fallen. But the police report that Megan found had very little information. The police ruled out foul play. So, theoretically, Holly wasn't pushed.

But the rest of the report confused Megan. An eye witness, a woman whose name was given, had seen the fall. According to her, the girl, Holly, was sitting on the railing when she leaned back and fell off. There was no information about a second person, Michelle, on the balcony at the time.

Megan tried to call the witness. Unfortunately, the woman was deceased. She would've been over 100.

64

Then Megan called the detective who had handled the case, Sergeant Antonelli. She dreaded calling him. But she got his voicemail.

Over the hours that followed she left several messages for him, but he never returned her calls.

Then she remembered that Victor was close to Sergeant Antonelli.

"He hasn't called me back yet," said Megan.

"He must be busy." Victor sighed. "He's a great guy. He trained me when I first started. One time my mother was really sick, and we had no insurance. He brought her food, paid for the medication, and even paid the hospital bill. I'll never forget that. He went out of his way to help my family."

Megan talked to Lieutenant Dodge about what happened at Twilight Towers.

"Oh yeah, I remember that incident," he said, polishing his badge. "As far as we know, she just fell. I think a witness saw her fall, right?"

Megan nodded.

"I didn't work that case, but I remember hearing the girl's name around town. She had a lot of personal problems. That's all I know."

When Megan looked up the owner of the condo online, she found that it was held by an offshore trust. It was transferred into the trust by a David Coda. She had heard that name before. It had some sort of bad connotation.

Megan went to the microfilm room at the station and found the few stories that came out in the paper at the time. It was the department's policy to keep on file any news story that mentioned the police. The stories were sparse and vague:

Teen Critical Following Accident

A teenager is in the intensive care unit at Memorial Hospital after falling from Twilight Towers, a condominium development.

Police responded to the complex yesterday after receiving several reports that someone had fallen from the roof. They rushed the victim, a female, to the hospital where she remains in critical condition.

Details of the incident are unavailable.

Girl, 16, Dies in fall from Twilight Towers

A fall from a porch balcony on Monday claimed the life of a sixteen-year-old girl, police say. According to Sergeant John Antonelli, the girl, identified as Holly O'Brien, fell from the third or fourth floor balcony of Twilight Towers, a condominium development. She was rushed to the hospital and died Wednesday morning.

The investigation is ongoing.

No Foul Play in Girl's Death

There is no evidence of foul play in the mysterious death of a teenage girl, according to police. The girl, Holly O'Brien, fell from the fourth floor of an apartment building last Monday.

Police spokesman Sergeant John Antonelli said the incident is still under investigation.

Victor came into the room. "So, did you find anything?"

"Not much. There was a girl named Holly, and she did fall, and she did die, but there's nothing to indicate she was pushed."

"Well, Michelle's crazy. Who knows what really happened."

"Victor, I have a feeling Michelle didn't push her at all."

Victor shrugged. "I don't know what to think. This is one of the strangest cases I've ever seen."

Megan and Victor went back in the room. Michelle was huddled in the corner. She got up and sat back down at the table.

They began to ask her a barrage of questions, one after the other:
"What time did it happen?"
"What was Holly wearing?"
"Where was Holly when you pushed her?"
"Why did you do it?"
On and on like that for half an hour.

Before Michelle could answer each question, they would ask another one. Then they tried to confuse her by changing her story and insisting she said something else.

"Where was Holly when you pushed her?" asked Victor.

"She was standing on the balcony railing."

"So *you* were standing on the balcony railing?" said Megan.

"No. Holly was."

"Wait a minute!" said Victor. "You just said *you* were on the railing too. Why are you changing your story?"

"I'm not."

"Yes you are!" yelled Megan.

Victor put his face up to Michelle's. His voice turned loud and angry. "You didn't answer me, Michelle! I asked you why you did it!"

Michelle burst into tears. "I told you, she kept calling me 'Little Girl'!"

Victor laughed. "That doesn't make sense. Why would that make you mad enough to kill her? What are you, a schizoid little freak?"

Megan looked at him. "Because she kept calling her that, over and over again, right Michelle?"

Michelle nodded. "I knew *he* wouldn't understand."

"Why, because I'm Spanish?" Victor laughed, winking at Megan.

"I do," said Megan. "I understand, Michelle."

"Last question, Michelle," said Victor. "Why wait over twenty years to tell us?"

Michelle sobbed even more. "Everything started to remind me of it! I kept hearing that song *Oysters In A Sandbox*! I hadn't heard it in over twenty years! That's the song that was playing when it happened! I kept imagining that different girls I saw were Holly! I

67

kept remembering her! I was having nightmares! I kept going to her grave! I went to the building and heard someone scream and saw her on the balcony! Megan, you saw me there! When I went up, she wasn't there! I pushed one of my students into a wall thinking she was Holly, and she that was hurting me, I mean, another girl. Nobody knows about it! Megan, you said I accosted that girl by the water! Then I went to The Caves looking for Holly and forgot where I was!"

When she mentioned The Caves, Megan looked away.

"But Michelle," said Megan, "you could get life in prison! There's no statute of limitation for murder!"

"I have to be punished for what I did to Holly! I can't live with it anymore!"

Megan and Victor left the room again.

"All we can do is write up our reports," said Victor.

"Victor, you saw how she was. She either couldn't remember the details, or she kept getting the facts wrong. This is really disturbing! I say we wait a little while!"

"Megan, the clock is ticking! We can't keep holding her unless we arrest her!"

"She hasn't asked to leave! She's here by choice, remember? Besides, there are a few things I want to check out."

"Like?"

"Like why wasn't the witness who saw Holly fall ever mentioned in the news stories?"

"Lag. A story is only hot once, unless it's definitely a murder or a high profile case. A week later, no one even remembers and reporters move on to other stories. Sometimes it takes a week to investigate, find people, take statements, and put it all together. By then everybody's forgotten about it. Ask any reporter."

"I also want to check out Twilight Towers and the guy who owns the condo. I live there for God's sake! Does the name David Coda sound familiar to you?"

Victor shrugged. "He's kind of a shady character. He used to let teenagers hang around his place all the time. Used to date teenage girls, even back when he was like fifty. You know what that probably means – drugs. But I don't think we've ever had a complaint about him."

"And since Michelle can't remember all the details, I say we bring in an investigative hypnotist."

Victor laughed. "That dude whose picture you drool over every day?"

She smiled and hit him playfully. "Yeah! Maybe he can help get to the truth by hypnotizing Michelle. It's worth a try."

Victor laughed again. "That stuff's fake! It's all a show! The Chief will never pay for it! And if he does, he's crazier than both you *and* the ice cream girl!"

"Chief," said Megan, "you've got to admit this is an unusual case, with unusual circumstances. Can we hire him?"

The Chief shook his head and pointed to the brochure. "His fees are way too high."

"What if I could get someone else to pay for it?"

"Who?"

"I'll let you know when I find out!"

"I want to stay here for the rest of the night." Michelle told Megan.

"Don't you want to call your husband?"

"I will, first thing in the morning. I'm too tired to face anybody tonight, and I know this will ruin him . . ."

"Okay, Michelle. I'll put you in protective custody."

Megan led her to the holding area.

Then Megan drove to Twilight Towers. She wanted to check out a theory she had.

She got off the elevator on the fourth floor and slinked through the hall to the balcony.

Looking at the railing, she realized it was not quite high enough for someone to hide behind, unless the person was very small. Though Michelle was short, she couldn't have been shorter than the railing and wall. So it was hard to believe that Michelle was there, had pushed someone, and that the witness hadn't reported it.

Did the witness not observe Michelle? Did Michelle hide after she pushed Holly? Megan didn't know what to think.

As she walked back to the door, Megan heard a scream, like that of a young girl. She turned around; nobody was there.

69

She searched the halls and the balconies of the other three floors and found nothing. Not a soul was about. It must have come from one of the apartments.

Then something happened to Megan.

THIRTEEN

"I'm going to tell everybody what you guys did!"

IT struck Megan hard. *It had happened at her building.* Two floors above, and down the porch from her door. That gave her the creeps.

The building always gave Megan an eerie sensation. Almost like the building didn't want her there.

She remembered the day she rented it. The view of the ocean on the back porch and the view of the street in the front. Not too far from the police station either.

Since she worked so many hours, she hardly ever saw her neighbors. This lack of human contact made the place seem even more distant and aloof.

Michelle's experience was all too familiar to Megan. The more she thought about it, the more she realized that. A mysterious fall. Doing drugs or drinking beforehand. Knowing for years and years that it was your fault. Not knowing what *really* happened. Living with those haunting memories. The nightmares. The flashbacks. Going back to where it happened and trying to understand it all.

Megan took a walk to the edge of the woods. Should she go in? Was she ready to face the memories of The Caves tonight?

Crack! Megan stepped on a twig. She pushed branches away that were just starting to bud. Soon they would all have green leaves and you wouldn't be able to see anything.

She kept walking, over the muddy grass, rocks, fallen branches, and leaves. It would be a miracle if she even found the place, since so many years had passed.

It began to get dark as twilight descended. Megan pressed on.

71

Finally, she saw it. It was in a clearing. It was even higher than she remembered: The Caves.

There were several levels and curved openings at each level, *like balconies without railings.*

A long time ago, she used to come here with Ryan and Matt. But that one night they brought Billy. Billy Kinecki. The school principal's son.

Poor Billy. No one saw him fall. Did he suffer?

Matt was tall and thin with styled black hair. He was a quiet, artistic boy, and he later became a doctor.

Ryan had curly brown hair and broad shoulders. He was a football player and he became a coach.

The last time she saw them was at their first high school reunion. They all stood around not knowing what to say to each other. Finally, they scattered and didn't talk again that night. That was four years ago.

Megan remembered the conversation with Billy Kinecki that had started the tragic chain of events. That conversation was like the spark that started the Chicago Fire.

"I hate this school!" he said. "Everybody has their own stupid little group and they don't want to talk to anybody else! It gets really aggravating . . ."

His pudgy face was red and his glasses were starting to fog. They were sitting in Math class and the teacher had given them the remaining few minutes to start the homework. Since they were allowed to work with partners, and since none of Megan's other friends were in that class, she chose Billy. Billy didn't seem to care if he had a partner or not. He had to do the homework, or the teacher would tell his father.

"What did you get for number nine?" asked Megan.

Billy looked down at his paper. "Y equals negative seven. Have you ever drunk beer, Megan?"

Most of the other kids were talking, so no one was really paying attention to Megan and Billy's conversation. Nonetheless, Megan looked around.

"Yep," she said.

"Yeah, right."

"Me and Ryan and Matt go to The Caves sometimes."

"THE CAVES!"

A group of kids at a table next to them stopped talking and looked.

"Be quiet!" whispered Megan. "We don't want anybody to find out!"

"I've had beer too!" said Billy. "I even have a regular buyer!"

Megan looked around. She recalled how she, Ryan, and Matt, had gone to great pains to get someone to buy the cases of beer for them. They would wait on the dark side of the strip mall. If they saw someone young about to go near the liquor store, one of them would approach him or her and offer to buy the person something in exchange. Sometimes they had to ask several people. They took turns asking.

Once, a young guy with a baseball cap on backwards took their money and drove off, not even going into the liquor store at all.

"Hey!" yelled Matt. "You bastard!"

"What are you going to do, call the police?" the young man laughed as he drove away.

Another night, when Ryan approached someone, the guy nodded over to where Megan and Matt were standing in the shadows. The man pointed to Megan.

Ryan suddenly pulled away from the guy and walked back to Megan and Matt. The man laughed and went in the store.

"What did he say?" asked Megan.

Ryan looked Megan up and down.

"You don't want to know!" he said.

"We can always use a buyer." Megan said to Billy. "Has he ever screwed you -- you know, taken your money and ran away?"

Billy shook his head.

"What did you get for number ten?"

The bell rang.

Megan kept making her way through the woods. She had no flashlight; that would give her away. So she relied on the full moon and the scattered lights from the houses that bordered the woods.

'They've sure built more houses here since I was a kid,' Megan thought.

And they were going to build a whole new housing development. Some developer had bought this land. He was going to blast away The Caves . . .

Megan's nose caught the scent of something burning, like a camp fire. Maybe the kids at The Caves had made one. Megan and her friends did that when they went there.

After stepping over the debris of an old stone wall, Megan caught sight of a glowing flame on the towering rock formation. She heard voices, low tones, whose words she couldn't make out.

Then the floodgate of memories broke. It was the scrunchie. She took off her scrunchie before she did it. Was it still there? Was it still lying under the same bush she threw it under?

Ryan. Matt. Billy. Poor Billy.

While Ryan and Matt were trying out for Pony League baseball, Billy was home building his models or playing games on his computer. Megan remembered that some of the other kids told him not to try out for sports because he was too short, too fat, and couldn't run fast.

"Have you ever eaten a whole big bag of chips at once?" Billy asked her.

"No! That's too much!"

"I have! And I drank a whole two-liter of Coke with it!"

Megan shook her head. That must be bad for you, she thought.

After school one day, Megan was walking with Ryan and Matt.

"Megan!" Billy said, running towards them. "Call me tonight! I'll give you all the answers to the homework!"

Ryan and Matt looked Billy up and down. Billy pushed his glasses back up his nose.

"Okay!" said Megan.

When Billy ran away, Matt and Ryan laughed.

"He likes you, Megan!" Ryan chuckled.

Megan felt herself blush.

"So?"

"So, he's a geek!" said Matt. "Plus, he's Kinecki's kid! Moe's own. That guy yells at me just for being two seconds late to homeroom!"

Megan heard the playful yell of a male voice on top of The Caves. Then she heard the crackle of a fire.

If only that night so long ago hadn't happened, she thought. What were they thinking? Drinking beer and sitting up on a high cliff like that?

Suddenly, in her mind, it was the day of the incident. *Megan was leaving the cafeteria with her friends.*

"Megan!" *Billy ran through the crowded hall to catch up to them. Someone tried to trip him.*

"Loser!" *someone yelled to him.*

"Faggot!" *someone else yelled.*

The two girls walking with Megan rolled their eyes and kept going. They had the same hip hairstyle as Megan and wore similar stylish clothes.

". . . are we still going to The Caves?" *Billy asked.*

Megan nodded. "You've got a buyer, right?"

"Yeah."

"Okay. Meet us at the edge of the woods, on that side street near the park – okay?"

Billy nodded.

". . . and don't tell anyone – and I mean anyone – got it!"

"Yeah."

Later, after school, Megan met up with Ryan and Matt.

"Billy Kinecki!?!?!" *said Matt.*

"Who cares!" *said Ryan.* "He can get us the beer!"

"Yeah, but he's got a big mouth!" *said Matt.* "What if he tells Mr. Kinecki?"

"He better not tell!" *said Megan,* "He knows he'll get picked on even more."

"But he'll be even more of a geek if he's drunk!" *said Matt.* "What if he passes out, or starts getting stupid!"

"We'll just tell him to shut up!" *said Megan.* "If he starts getting too bad we can take the beer away from him. You guys can even beat him up – he knows that!"

"We can even take off and leave him, once we get the beer," *said Ryan.* "He can't run! He'll never find us in those woods!"

"Okay," *said Matt.* "But he better not do anything stupid!"

That night, Matt, Megan, and Ryan waited on a park bench near the edge of the woods. Then along came Billy, pulling a little red wagon with something on it, wrapped up in a blanket.

Megan remembered being embarrassed. Ryan and Matt rolled their eyes.

"Did you get it?" asked Matt.

Billy pushed his glasses back up his nose. "Yep."

Ryan pointed to the wagon. "This thing will never make it through the woods – we'll have to carry the beer."

When they got to The Caves, there were only three other kids there smoking crack. But they left early.

Megan, Ryan, Matt, and Billy drank the beer. They played the portable CD player/radio. And they drank. And they drank some more. And they talked, mostly about school, the teachers, and the other kids. Then they had even more beer.

Matt and Ryan got rambunctious as they climbed up on the rocks near the edge, jumping around, jostling each other, yelling.

Billy came close to Megan, who was stirring up the fire with a stick.

"Megan?" he whispered. "Have you ever done it?"

"Done what?"

"It!"

"Are you asking me if I've ever had sex?"

"Yeah."

"Gross! It's none of your business anyway!"

"I have!"

"Yeah, right."

"You'll never believe with who!"

"I don't even care, Billy."

"It was one of the teachers!"

Megan laughed out loud. "Shut up, Billy!"

He smiled knowingly and went away.

It got later and later. Matt and Ryan started acting crazier and crazier, wrestling and jostling each other even more. Then they started jostling Megan.

Matt started putting his hands on Megan. At first, just patting her back or patting his hand on her shoulder. Then they were holding hands. Then he had his arm around her.

Billy was passed out near some bushes. He didn't see it happen, she thought.

She remembered feeling beautiful, and loved the fact that both Ryan and Matt found her hot. So, soon she was necking with Ryan, who she liked better anyway. Then his lips moved down her neck, and he was feeling her breasts. She liked that. Then he had her bra off, and he was feeling her butt and legs as they lay in some soft grass.

She pulled off the scrunchie that held her hair in a bun. When she tossed it into some bushes, it fell to the ground and would stay there for a long time.

Megan was concerned. Should she say no? Ryan was sweating, working on her like a madman. He was hard and ready. She wanted his affection, but she just wasn't sure of more, not yet.

Slowly, carefully, while licking her breasts, he took her pants down. He was on top of her now, undoing his fly and button.

"Ah, Ryan . . ." she said softly.

He was just too wild to hear her, or understand. He eased into her. Once. Twice. Three times. She wrapped her legs around his body so she could feel it tighter and tighter. And she moaned.

She felt a rush, a high, and a burst of wildness that she had never experienced in her life!

Then everything went into overdrive. One thing led to another. She felt tears on her cheek. She wasn't sad, she was a little scared, but most of all she felt beautiful, like she had never felt before in her life. Electrified. It was like riding the biggest rollercoaster at Six Flags – STANDING UP! It was terrifying, electrifying, adrenaline-surging – oh, what a rush!

Then it was Matt's turn. Wow. Nobody had planned it. It was just happening. Matt was cute, but he wasn't as powerful as Ryan. Since she didn't want to hurt Matt's feelings, she had to pretend she was getting off. So she let out a loud scream that echoed through the woods.

Ryan sat on a rock mumbling. ". . . homerun . . . oh, baby, homerun . . ."

Megan woke up. No. She wasn't dreaming. There was Matt, sitting on the ground next to her trying to catch his breath while wiping the sweat off his head. And there was Ryan, pulling up his pants, zipping his fly.

Wow. What a night.

A thought struck Megan. Billy must still be passed out in the bushes.

Then she felt someone touch her hair and a wet kiss on her lips. It was Billy. He tried to kiss her again, his lips puckered.

"Billy!" Megan yelled.

She was just too tired to do it again. First it was one. Then it was two. Now three? No! Not three! What if anyone found out it was one?

"I love you Megan!" Billy touched her breasts awkwardly.

"Billy, STOP!"

It must have been like getting shot. Billy's head hung low and she knew there were tears welling up under his glasses.

"But Megan, I love you! Those two don't love you! They just wanted you for your body! I care about you! We could be happy together! We don't have to tell anybody! I won't say anything! So, is it you and me or what?"

It was pathetic. The whine and crack in his voice. The pleading. He was a little boy suddenly trying to be a man by using corny lines. She felt bad for Billy, but she also felt disgusted. Ryan and Matt were men. Billy was a little boy. He voice hadn't even changed yet.

It would be like riding the biggest, wildest rollercoaster at Six Flags – standing up. And then going on the kiddy carousel afterwards.

"Come on, Megan, just once! Please! I'll give you all the answers to the homework!"

"Shut up, Billy!" said Ryan.

"Get out of here, Billy!" said Matt.

Billy staggered. He could barely stand up. The beer had taken its toll on all of them.

"I hate you! I hate all of you! It's not fair! I'm the one who got the beer! I'm going to tell everybody what you guys did!"

The last sentence echoed in their minds. 'I'm going to tell everybody what you guys did.'

Billy was gone.

"Stop him!" Megan became hysterical. "EVERYBODY WILL KNOW!"

There was no plan. Nobody knew what to do, because they were all drunk and it was almost pitch black. Matt went one way, Ryan the other, and Megan, a different way.

The last thing Megan remembered was some sort of commotion in the distance, the rustling of bushes and some yelling. She couldn't make out who was yelling. Then she heard a cry; a primal scream in the night. Then a loud thud. That was it.

Somehow, they all met up near the edge of the woods later. No one said anything. Megan remembered seeing the little red wagon Billy had hidden under the park bench.

They just looked at each other and knew. And they never talked about it again, except the next day at the police station.

"How did Billy Kinecki fall?"

Sergeant Antonelli had his face up to Megan's in the dim interrogation room. Her parents, on either side of her, were too shocked to speak.

Megan sobbed. Tears ran down her cheek.

"I don't know!"

"Yeah, you do! What were you doing drinking up there! We found forty-eight empty beer cans! Just tell us how he fell and you can go home!"

"My daughter says she didn't see it happen!" said her mother. "She knows she shouldn't have been drinking – she'll be severely punished for that – but she didn't see that boy fall!"

"Who got you the beer?" asked Sergeant Antonelli.

"I don't know!" said Megan. "Someone brought it! I don't remember who!"

Sergeant Antonelli shook his head. "We'll find out! Whoever did will get twenty years for this!"

They had to let her go. It was hell at her house after that. She was grounded and couldn't do anything, not even watch TV. And she wasn't allowed to see any of her friends or go anywhere. The same thing happened to Ryan. But Matt's mother, a single mom who worked two jobs, wasn't able to keep that tight a rein on him, and he still had the most freedom.

Megan had an idea about what happened, but she wasn't sure. She thought Matt might've pushed Billy off. He was the most opposed to Billy and picked on him the most. But she didn't know for sure.

Now it was starting to haunt her again, only more so now. Did Ryan know? Did Ryan push him? Did Billy just fall by accident?

Megan began to think she would never find out. But whatever happened, it was her fault. If she had just given in to Billy, he would still be alive today. If she had just given him some attention, then he would be alive today. If she had just pretended to like him, more than just as a friend, he would still be alive today.

She thought of all the pleasures he could have enjoyed. All of life's experiences he had missed out on. All of life's pleasures she had enjoyed, but with a trace of guilt always. That's why she couldn't be happy, or stay in a relationship. That's why she hid behind her job. It was the guilt.

Megan climbed to the top of The Caves. No one was there. Did she just imagine the fire and the voices?

She looked over the edge. It was a long way down. She could see the lights from the town in the distance.

Then she backed up several yards and ran as fast as she could. *Megan threw herself off The Caves.*

Megan jolted awake. She was in her own bed. Kit Kat leaped in the air and let out a loud hiss and MEOW! She had scared him when she jumped awake.

Megan's heart beat like a war drum. She broke out in sweat.

Megan turned the lights and TV on. She tried to sleep. But Megan didn't get any more sleep that night.

FOURTEEN

"Something really bad happened at the condo that day."

EVEN with the light and TV on, Megan could only doze off and wake up every few minutes. She couldn't stop thinking about Michelle, Billy, and Holly.

She woke up to an infomercial hawking some retro music CD. A song called *Oysters In A Sandbox* was playing: *"Now you find yourself alone since '82/Now I find myself with the memories of you/With no sand to hide/The lost trace of time/And all those dreams you had/When your eyes were barely green/And all those things we did/Looking back I should've seen /That deep down you cared/I just wish you were here/Oysters in a sandbox . . ."*

Ouch! Megan thought. Did that singer know what she was going through?

Megan looked around the walls of her apartment. Her cell was bigger than Michelle's, but it was a cell nonetheless. At least she could come and go as she wished. Michelle was locked up.

Kit Kat woke up and stretched. She petted him and he purred even more. Then he curled back up into a ball.

While she had Kit Kat, Michelle had a husband. Megan did not. She wanted a man so very badly, but with so many hours on the job . . . men afraid of a woman with a badge . . . too much emotional baggage from the past . . . guilt . . .

Megan looked at the clock. Six AM.

She picked up her phone and called Ryan. He didn't answer. She left him a message. He probably wasn't even up yet.

Then she called Matt. Megan had left several messages on his voicemail, but he hadn't returned her calls. He never answered the phone; but that morning was different.

". . . hello . . ." said a tired male voice, probably awakened.

"Matt! How's it going! It's Megan! Megan Downs!"

"Oh, yeah. Hey, look, I've been real busy, sorry I haven't called you back . . ."

"It's okay, Matt. So, how are you doing?"

"Oh, fine, I guess. I'm putting in a lot of hours at the hospital right now. Residency. I was just sleeping. Hey, can I call you back . . ."

"Matt, do you ever think about it?"

Silence.

"Think about what?"

"That night at The Caves, with Billy . . ."

Silence.

"Megan, I think we better let that one rest. It was a long time ago for chrissakes! Get over it! We can't bring Billy back! He's dead!"

"Yeah. Do you have nightmares about it? I do."

Silence.

"God, Megan, it's really early. I . . ."

"Matt, did you see it happen? Did you see him go over the edge?"

"NO! Nobody saw it happen! Don't you remember? It was dark! He ran off! He just fell! That's all! He just fell! Goodbye, Megan!"

Click. Silence.

Kit Kat meowed. It was time to feed her best friend.

Megan called two of her female friends. They weren't up yet either. More voicemail. More unreturned calls. So Megan fell asleep for a few minutes.

Waking up groggy, Megan played with a couple of Teddy Bears from her collection. There was the white one holding a heart that she got for Valentine's Day one year. There was the cute little thumb-sucking bear she had sent away for. There was her family of Koala bears – Mom, Dad, two cubs. Mike the polar bear. Panda bear. The mean, but cute polar bear. Bill the Grizzly Bear. Benny the Brown Bear. Then there was just plain old brown Teddy, her favorite. She got him for Christmas, from her grandmother, when she was two years old. Megan picked him up and hugged him.

Then the sun began to rise. She had a strange thought.

She picked up her favorite Teddy Bear, Teddy. Then she got dressed.

Megan braided her hair into pigtails – just to be different.

The officer on desk duty was surprised to see Megan come in with a Teddy Bear.

"What's this?" he asked. "Is it 'Toys for Tots' time already?"

Megan smiled and shook her head. She got a bottle of water from the vending machine.

She went to the holding area. Michelle was wide awake and sitting up.

Megan opened the cell and handed her the water and the Teddy Bear.

"I thought you might want some company, Michelle."

Michelle stared at the bear, then at Megan, and then hugged the bear. She started to cry.

Megan sat down next to her and hugged her, stroking Michelle's snarled, dirty hair.

"Thank you, Megan."

"You're welcome."

Michelle looked into Megan's big, gentle, understanding brown eyes as Megan spoke.

"Michelle, I was very worried about you. I couldn't sleep."

Michelle nodded as she drank the water.

"Michelle, can I ask you, why did you quit teaching all of a sudden? Everybody says you were a great teacher!"

Michelle gulped the water down. "Because Holly loved the ice cream truck. That's what she wanted to do. If she couldn't be happy, she wanted to make other people happy."

"So, you were kind of carrying a torch for Holly?"

Michelle looked away.

"I can relate to what you're going through," Megan said. "You see, when I was younger, in 8th Grade, my friends and I used to go partying at The Caves. We thought we were so big! Just a bunch of stupid kids!"

"So were we," said Michelle.

"Then one night, we went a little too far. We drank way too much . . . then Billy was going to tell on us, and we all ran after him . . . I don't know what happened . . . but he fell . . . or someone pushed him . . . I'll never know."

"Mr. Kinecki's son?"

"Yeah!"

"Oh my God!"

Megan burst into tears.

Michelle looked away. "We went too far at the condo . . . on acid . . ."

"Michelle, are you sure you pushed Holly?"

"Yeah."

"You said Holly kept calling you 'Little Girl.' Were you mad because she never validated you?"

Michelle sobbed. "She used to hurt me. Physically, it was okay, because it didn't happen that much and she was always sorry. She was like a big sister or a mother to me; always there to protect me. My own mother never had a clue about life!

"Holly saved me so many times. Like when the popular girls used to harass me, or the boys used to come on too strong when they got drunk . . . and one day she came to me, crying. I thought she was so grown up. Like a woman. But she was just a frightened child – like me! She wouldn't stop crying. She made me promise to always be her friend. I told her she was using drugs too much."

"So, the roles were reversed?"

"Yeah!"

"But Michelle, you say you pushed Holly off the railing? Why would you do that if she was always there to help you?"

Michelle wailed. "I wouldn't have taken drugs if it weren't for her! I wouldn't be throwing up on heroin if it weren't for her! I wouldn't be up in that condo if it weren't for her! I wouldn't be on LSD if it weren't for her! I wouldn't be failing in school if it weren't for her! I wouldn't be getting in trouble in school if it weren't for her! My mother and father wouldn't have threatened to send me away to DYS if it weren't for her! All these guys wouldn't be touching me if it weren't for her!"

"So," said Megan, "you just pushed her off the balcony when you had your chance?"

"Yeah! She called me 'Little Girl!' I hated when she called me that! I told her never to call me that again! I wasn't a little girl!

Guys were touching me! I could smoke and drink! I took LSD! And she still called me 'Little Girl!' Don't you see?"

Michelle's eyes turned yellow with anger and she gritted her teeth.

Megan sighed. "But Michelle, a witness saw her fall off! And the witness didn't mention someone pushing her! How do you explain that?"

"Holly got up on the railing. She said: 'I can fly Shelly! I can fly!' I told her to get down from there or she'd fall. She said: 'I can fly little girl! Come fly with me!' I went to go back in the condo, and pushed her legs. She fell."

"But why didn't the witness see you?"

"The balcony wall was high, and I'm so short . . ."

"You couldn't have been that short. I measured it. You would have to be less than four feet tall not to be seen."

"I pushed Holly off! That's just the way it is!"

Megan looked at Michelle. There was a time, at the police station, when she was fourteen, when she almost wanted to tell them that she had pushed Billy, even though she hadn't. Then she would be punished and not feel guilty. As it turned out, she had felt guilty all this time. Megan almost envied Michelle's freedom of being able to admit to something like that.

Megan turned to leave. As she did, Michelle hugged her. Megan hugged her back.

"Something really bad happened at the condo that day." Michelle sobbed.

"What, Michelle?"

"Megan, I can't remember! This guy came in! He did something!"

"Did you block it out?"

"I think so! It was terrible!"

"Michelle, sometimes when people can't remember something they can get hypnotized. It helps them remember. Would you like to get hypnotized?"

"No! It wouldn't work, anyway."

"You don't know that."

"No!"

Megan decided to take another approach to the situation. She remembered her high school acting class.

"Let me be honest with you, Michelle. You might be mentally ill. If you are, and they charge you with murder, the court could order you to be put in a mental hospital until you're able to stand trial! I've seen you do some pretty strange things myself. Do you know what Bridgewater State is like? Let me tell you! They put you on drugs all day and turn you into a zombie! Then they wrap you up in freezing cold wet sheets for hours just to keep you calm! Then they strap you to a table and plug you into the wall! If not, they'll saw open your skull and take a piece out of your brain! You'll be wearing diapers and have to learn how to walk and talk again!

"Have you ever read about Bridgewater State in the paper? Rats the sizes of small dogs run through the place and bite you while you sleep! That's *if* you can sleep! It's hard when people are screaming twenty-four hours a day! People have been killed there! They've found skeletons buried outside! The patients piss on the floor! The attendants abuse the patients, especially females . . .."

"STOP!" yelled Michelle.

Megan caught her breath. "Michelle, you may have pushed Holly, but even if you're punished for that, you'll never be free unless you come face to face with what happened at the condo that day! You know that yourself!"

Michelle covered her face, sobbing. She stood up and paced around the cell.

"You'll be treated fairly, Michelle. I'll see to that. If you let us hypnotize you, I'll see to it personally that you don't go to Bridgewater State. I'll put my life and badge on the line for that."

"Are you sure?" Michelle looked into Megan's eyes.

"Michelle, I give you my word. Nothing bad will happen to you. It will be over my dead body. And I don't plan on dying soon."

"I want to talk to my husband first."

"Okay. We'll call him right now."

Michelle lay down on the bunk, cuddling Teddy. Megan sat at her feet.

"Megan, you're so pretty. You must have been really popular in school."

Megan blushed. "I never really thought about it."

"What was it like, being popular?"

Megan shrugged. "I don't know. You have to wear the right clothes and have the right hairstyle. You can't say the wrong thing at the wrong time, or talk to the wrong people, and if you do, you have to pretend they don't matter to you . . ."

Megan sighed. "It's like being on a treadmill. You have to keep up. You keep moving but you don't go anywhere."

"Megan, when you were in school, did you ever make fun of kids who weren't popular? I mean, at my job, I see so many lonely kids. Kids who don't fit in. Kids who walk home from school all alone. It makes me so sad sometimes."

"I know what you mean. I don't think I ever made *fun* of anybody . . . But I should've spoken up more, like when they picked on Billy. Yes, he was my friend. But I couldn't say it.

"I wanted to say something when I saw other kids getting picked on, but I was too afraid. That's one thing about being 'popular.' You're always afraid you suddenly won't be anymore. You lose part of yourself.

"I don't think I really was *that* popular. I'm just good at talking to people. I can 'relate.' I listen. I look you in the eye when you talk. A lot of people don't. 'Popularity' is all relative anyway. It's all in degrees. You don't realize what things are like, and what you have, until you've passed that point."

"Megan, why did you become a cop, I mean, you seem so nice . . ."

Megan laughed. "My parents wanted me to go to law school. So I took criminal justice classes. I promised them I would have a career in law, I just didn't tell them to what extent! I was a rebel. I wanted to do things *my* way. Work on my own. And I guess I just fell into it. Maybe protect people. People like Billy. Then it got in my blood and now I hide behind my job! I'd trade my job for a man any day!"

Megan got up to leave.

"Megan, thank you. Thank you for everything."

A short time later, Michelle called Rick. That started a whole new chain of events – mostly bad.

FIFTEEN

"Holly thought she could fly and I pushed her off. She made me mad. She was ruining my life. She kept calling me Little Girl."

MICHELLE called Rick. She told him what happened. He dropped the phone.

Half an hour later, Rick arrived at the police station. So did his attorney, Ed Stark. Attorney Stark had a long, thick beard, and wore a leather jacket over a prayer shawl.

He rode on a Harley Davidson that was so loud it numbed the eardrums of everybody within two miles.

His helmet was shaped like a yarmulke.

Having won a high profile settlement after suing the State Police, Stark's license was up for review on an ethics violation. He was known as a ". . . ruthless Barracuda . . ."

Victor and Megan looked at each other and cringed when he came in the door.

Then Megan, Michelle, Victor, Rick, and Attorney Stark met in a conference room. There was a video screen set up on the table.

Michelle's face was pale and her eyes were red. Her hair was going in every direction.

Rick hugged Michelle and she buried her face in his chest.

"Thank God you're alright!" he said. "I can't believe this is happening!"

"We're at a Mexican standoff," said Victor. "We're not sure whether or not to file murder charges. It all depends on how this meeting goes."

Rick lunged at Victor. Attorney Stark and Megan held him back.

"You're an asshole!" yelled Rick. "Michelle didn't kill anybody!"

"Yes I did," said Michelle. "It's about time I got punished."

Rick looked at Attorney Stark. "They're setting her up! They got her to admit to something she never did! Michelle wouldn't do that!"

"Even after taking LSD?" asked Megan.

Michelle twitched her wrist. "Holly thought she could fly and I pushed her off. She made me mad. She was ruining my life. She kept calling me Little Girl."

"Can I be honest?" said Attorney Stark. "You can't make Michelle testify against herself, and I can get that so-called confession statement she wrote thrown out of court for a hundred different reasons. You cops shouldn't make yourselves look even more stupid than you really are. Just drop this case so you can go back to drinking your coffee, hassling innocent people and wasting taxpayers' money. That's all you're good for anyway."

"Don't flatter us!" said Megan, "We've heard it all before! Don't you think we should find out what happened at the condo that day?"

"Yes!" said Michelle.

"NO!" said Rick. "I remember the news stories. Nobody knows what really happened! Two teenage girls took drugs and one thought she could fly! It's happened to hundreds of people who took LSD!"

"Rick, haven't you noticed Michelle's been acting strange lately?" said Megan. "Wandering around late at night, twitching her wrist, and thinking other girls are Holly?"

Rick sighed. "Everybody goes through stuff like this . . . come on, Michelle! You know you didn't push Holly!"

"YES I DID!" she screamed. "Why won't anybody believe me! Why would I say it if it weren't true!"

"Is Michelle under arrest?" asked Attorney Stark.

"Yes!" yelled Megan. "We have a signed confession for a murder! I'll call the DA and we'll arraign her tomorrow morning – unless . . ."

"Unless what?" said Rick.

Megan spoke softly and gently. "I want her to be hypnotized by an investigative hypnotist."

"So you can put her away for murder?" Rick shook his head.

"No," said Megan. "So we can find out what really happened at the condo that day."

"Something really bad happened!" Michelle broke into sobs. "Before I pushed Holly off. Something really bad happened!"

"Don't say another word!" said Attorney Stark.

"Michelle blocked it out. Or the LSD did," said Megan. "Back in the '80's that building was known for shady stuff, like drugs. I want to get to the truth once and for all. Let's hypnotize Michelle!"

Attorney Stark laughed. "Not on your life! I won't allow my client to convict herself!"

Michelle kept twitching her wrist. "Everybody needs to stop calling me Michelle, and start calling me *Shelly*. I want to get hypnotized! Then I'll see Holly again!"

Rick glared at Megan. "That's what you cops do? Play on people's weaknesses to brainwash them? Just to make a case?"

"Let me show you something," said Megan.

She pressed the remote control and Dunn's video brochure started to play on the screen.

Wearing a black leather coat, blue jeans, and cowboy boots, he came into view from behind a tree. Then he stared into the camera for a minute. Everybody stared back. They became focused on his eyes, and he looked into their eyes, into their brains, through their hearts, and into their souls. They were spellbound.

Just like you reading this right now. Whenever you read a book this happens. As you are reading along, you begin to be aware of certain things. As you read, you suddenly become aware of the unique darkness and shape of the letters. And as you become aware of this, you can also see the contrasting whiteness of the page. And you can also become aware of the smoothness of the paper. And as you become aware of that, you can also feel the rise and fall of your chest as you breathe, and the slightest little nodding, little nodding of your head. And as your eyes begin to close . . .

Dunn took a cigarette pack from an inner pocket of his coat, took a cigarette out, put it in his mouth, and lit it with a pipe lighter.

"People, people, people," he finally spoke, blowing smoke out his nose. "You're watching this because you have a problem. What's the problem? Why all the trouble?

"Let me tell you something. I don't like any of you. In fact, I *hate* some of you. I have a job to do, and someone is going to pay me a lot of money, so I'll do the best I can."

He pointed to the camera. "I know all about you. Some things I found out about you people make me sick. But that's okay. Because the truth will come out anyway. Whether you like it or not.

"You may be wondering who I am, and why I can do the things I do. The truth is I have federal diplomatic immunity! I can commit any crime I want in the world short of murder, and that, too, if I smoke the right person! Let me repeat that so that it sinks into your tiny, stupid little heads. I can commit any crime I want and get away it! *If* they can even catch me! Just ask your lame-ass police department, and about fifty others! I'm above the law! Yet I *am* the law!

"See, I'm what the government calls a Level 5. A hired gunslinger that gets the job done. Who doesn't care. Who'll do anything I'm told. So they have to pay me money and give me special privileges and other things just to keep me happy! There are less than 100 of us in the country. We get called in to do certain jobs that nobody else can do! We know about things in the world that nobody else knows, or would even believe if we told you! And if we get too far out of control, someone kills us! And they make someone else a Level 5!"

He took several drags off his cigarette.

"Me, my name is Dunn. I don't care if you know my name. I have twelve aliases anyway. And I'm always moving around, so don't bother trying to find me!

"Let me tell you a little story. You see, years ago I went into law enforcement. I was well-trained and joined the tactical team of the U.S. Marshals. One of the reasons I wanted to be in law enforcement was because of what happened to my father. He was a rich man and we lived well. We had a farm in Ohio, swimming pool, big house, ten cars, domestic help, and every toy you could ever want.

"Our Dad made us work. He gave us food and clothes. The rest we had to earn.

"But there was this politician in our state who thought my father was too rich, and got him in trouble. They charged him with Tax Evasion, Land Fraud, and all kinds of other things he never did.

"They gave him a mock trial, probably threatened his own lawyer if he didn't lose the case, and put my father in the state penitentiary. There he got stabbed to death. They never found out who did it. (Yeah, right.)

"My family lost everything. We went bankrupt. Boo-hoo.

"So that's why I went into law enforcement. So that I could catch the same type of son-of-a-bitch that did my father in. So I could protect the innocent from evil.

"I get paid very well for what I do. But it's not about the money anymore. I have more money than I know what to do with. These days I mostly give to charities. And I pay my people well. I have everything I want. Not like you people who are trapped in the rat race until the day you die, which could very well be today!

"If you want the truth, then hire Dunn. I deliver."

Attorney Stark laughed. "Where's his trench coat and snap-brimmed hat?"

"Rick, please let them do it!" said Michelle.

"Do you really think it will help you?" he asked.

She nodded.

"But I don't want you to go to prison!" Tears welled in his eyes.

"I'll only allow it if the police agree in writing not to use anything against Michelle in court," said Attorney Stark.

"On one condition," said Megan. "Your client pays the hypnotist. He charges a really high fee."

Rick nodded. "Fine. Michelle's worth it."

Michelle smiled for the first time in days.

Much to Rick's disappointment, Michelle agreed to stay in protective custody.

"I just can't cope with anything right now . . ." she told him.

"We could arrest her," said Megan. "But as long as she agrees to stay we won't. After the hypnotist comes, we'll have to either charge her or let her go."

After everyone left the room, Rick and Michelle had a talk.

"Michelle, why didn't you tell me first?"

"I wanted to. I tried. I just couldn't. I knew it would destroy you!"

He held her face in his hands.

"Michelle, do you remember the night we met?"

She nodded, dripping tears from her cheeks.

"It was at the old Bentley School and me and my friend Danny came to see the volleyball game!"

Michelle smiled. "I was the worst volleyball player in the world! I lost the game for my team . . ."

"And do you remember what happened after the game, when one of those girls pushed you into the banister post and you cut your arm?"

Michelle gasped. "I thought that happened in 8th Grade! I keep getting things wrong!"

"Well, you were being harassed back then, like you are now. But then it was easy to help you. This whole thing's a lot harder. But we're going to get you out! I'll give my life if I have to!"

"Rick, just promise me you'll take care of yourself. I know I did it. I killed Holly. I have to be punished . . . but please come visit me . . ."

"Michelle, I don't think you . . ."

"JUST SAY YOU WILL!"

"I will Michelle. I promise."

Megan led Michelle back to the holding area.

Later, Megan emailed Dunn. He asked her to send him all the information she had on the case. He agreed to come in three days. Then he did even more research on his own.

Megan went to see many of the people Michelle had contact with on a daily basis. One of them was Mr. Kinecki. She dreaded doing it, but she realized she had to. They met in his office.

"I just wanted to get a few facts straight," said Megan. "Did you ever see any strange behavior from the ice cream girl, Michelle, when she used to work here?"

He shrugged. "Not really. Why?"

Megan could feel the tension building.

"I can't talk about it too much," she said. "It's something that happened years ago."

"Well . . . is that it?"

Megan nodded. Should she ask him? Something made her.

"One more question, Mr. Kinecki. What do you think happened to Billy the night he died?"

Mr. Kinecki stood up. "How dare you! How dare you mention my son's name! You! Of all people! You degenerate, juvenile delinquent! You, Megan Downs, were a troublemaker who used boys to get what you wanted! Drugs! Alcohol! Sex! And now what are you, a cop! A hypocrite! You sit in my office with a holier-than-thou attitude, when you were taking drugs and drinking right in this very building! Then you and your delinquent friends take my boy to the woods and you get him drunk and he falls off a cliff and dies! How dare you, you BITCH! GET THE HELL OUT OF MY OFFICE, NOW! I'M GOING TO TELL YOUR CHIEF! GET OUT, NOW! I CAN'T STAND THE SIGHT OF YOU!"

Dunn studied the pages Megan had scanned and emailed. What he read shocked him. Especially the address. Twilight Towers. *He knew the guy who owned the condo.*

Later that day, Megan's cell phone rang. The caller ID said 'Anonymous', so she didn't answer. But whoever was trying to reach her kept calling, over and over again. On the seventh or eighth time, Megan answered. It was Dunn.
"How did you get my cell number?"
"I have access to all the information in the world. Let me tell you, there is something bigger going on here. I *know* there is. It involves that building and the girl who fell from it. It involves your friend Billy. Yeah, I know all about that too. And it involves someone we've been trying to catch for years. Let's work together on this. Let's put some bad people away."
"I owe my loyalty to the department I work for."
"I'm not asking you to do anything you shouldn't. Believe me. Your chief is a good contact of mine. I've helped him before and he's helped me. He likes you. He'll back you up. You're not alone here . . ."
Either he hung up, or they lost the connection.

Driving home after leaving the police station, Rick's mind had begun to wander. Then a thought struck him. He had to talk to several people.

SIXTEEN

"Only a punk would walk that way!"

THE harrowing series of events that occurred next could've been avoided. Rick panicked. That's all. Either that or fear just got to him.

Searching through an old list of town residents, Rick looked up Holly's family. He realized they had lived next door to Jimmy Jendron, the owner of a construction company that Rick had hired to work on several of his buildings.

Now in his forties, Jimmy Jendron was a tall, thin, athletic man with wavy black hair and a wise-guy smirk. He had pock marks on his left cheek.

Jimmy's company always seemed to win large government building contracts. Rick had heard rumors that he was tied to organized crime. But Rick never believed it.

Rick called him, and they met the next morning. Wearing hardhats, they walked around the construction site of a new senior housing complex that Jimmy's company was building. Workers passed them carrying lumber, pushing wheelbarrows, and unloading trucks.

"Michelle's in big trouble. They might charge her with murder."

Jimmy's eyes opened wide. "I'm really sorry to hear that."

"Jimmy, what do you know about Holly O'Brien and the O'Brien family, your former neighbors?"

Jimmy seemed nervous. He became antsy and avoided eye contact.

"Do you know anything about how Holly might have fallen?" asked Rick. "I mean, you lived right next door to her . . ."

"I knew her father pretty well. Nice guy. But the family split up right after it happened. I bought their old house a couple years back and knocked it down. Built apartments on the lot. Made a good profit too. Sold fast."

"The whole incident was definitely mysterious, very little coverage in the paper. It just didn't add up. How do you think she fell?"

Jimmy shrugged. "I don't know. But there were a lot of rumors about it."

"What kind of rumors?"

Jimmy froze, as if he had said something he shouldn't have. He looked all around. "I can't talk about it!"

"Why?"

"How would you like it if your daughter got killed, and people kept asking questions! Would you want everybody spreading rumors?"

"Jimmy, I wouldn't normally ask this! Michelle could go to jail! What do you know about Holly?"

Jimmy shook his head. "If you keep asking questions, you're going to end up dead like her! That's what I know!"

Jimmy turned away and hurried across the street. He got in his car.

"Jimmy, wait!"

He didn't turn around.

Later that day, thumbing through a phone book, Rick looked up Holly's father. He dialed the number, and then hung up, afraid. Then he called it again. An older man answered.

After stuttering and stammering for several seconds, Rick finally managed to introduce himself. It was indeed Holly's father. Apparently, he didn't realize Holly had known Michelle.

"Sir," said Rick, "my wife was very good friends with your daughter. I don't know how to say this, but she thinks she pushed your daughter off the porch that day she fell. I don't believe it happened like that. Do you?"

The silence on the phone line was deafening.

"Is this a prank?"

"No sir, it certainly isn't. I wouldn't do that to anybody, especially under these circumstances. Do you think someone *pushed* your daughter off?"

"That's . . . not . . . what the cops said . . ." he muttered slowly and deliberately.

Rick was amazed by how well Holly's father maintained his composure.

". . . a lady saw her fall off, I thought . . ." he sighed.

"I'm really sorry to be asking you this . . . Michelle thought very highly of your daughter. She was a good friend. I can't even tell you how sorry I am about what happened to her."

Rick never forgot what the man said next.

"Both of my daughters were the sweetest, happiest, most beautiful little girls any father could ever hope for. Smart too. I was so proud! But then life was cruel to them." He fought back tears. "When they were little, they shared all their toys with all the other kids, and gave away everything. They loved everybody. They wanted to kiss everybody." He laughed. "I still have a picture of Holly in a purple dress, with yellow ribbons in her hair, kissing a little boy her age from Sunday school. But judging by the look on the boy's face, I don't think he was ready to be kissed by a girl yet!"

Holly's father started to cry. "It was like my girls knew no evil. They were always laughing and enjoying life. God, they cared more about everybody else than they did about themselves! Not a selfish bone in either one of them!"

Rick listened intensely.

"They were so different from the other kids, that the other kids couldn't understand them. Couldn't relate to them. Too much love. Too much generosity. Too sincere. Too naïve and pure. So the other kids made fun of my little girls!" he sobbed.

"Oh, they made some friends," he said. "But most of their so-called friends were the kind of kids who just took what they could get and used people. Most of them just used my girls.

"So my daughters became real close to each other. But more and more, year after year, the bitterness started setting in. My girls weren't happy anymore. They were finding out more and more how mean other kids can be, especially in their early teens! So they turned to drugs and alcohol. I never even knew how bad it was until years later.

"My wife was in complete denial. She never dealt with it. Before I knew it, we weren't a family anymore. Holly hardly ever came home. When she did, she was either drunk or high on drugs. My other daughter, Tammy, wouldn't come out of her room. Except to buy drugs. When she did, she started hanging around with criminals. My wife blamed me for everything! That hurt. We'd go days and weeks not speaking to each other. Do you know what that's like? Living in a house with three other people and not speaking to each other for two months?"

"It must've been really hard!"

"Oh, it was. I tried to talk some sense into Holly. Over and over again. I tried to tell her how beautiful she was, how smart she was, and what a wonderful future she had – if she straightened out. But she wouldn't listen. She shut me out completely.

"You know, Holly used to play the viola. She could even play Mozart! And she painted beautiful pictures. I still have some of them. Always with bright colors and people smiling. But she stopped all that once the drugs and alcohol took over.

"My other daughter thought I favored Holly. My wife wanted me to handle everything. Finally, one day, I couldn't take it anymore. The lies, the deception, the self destruction. So I threw my Holly, my baby girl, out of the house! I thought it would do her some good, you know, surviving on her own for a little while. But look what happened! It got her killed!" he broke down, sobbing.

"Well, you can't blame yourself. It sounds like you really tried. Michelle loved your daughter. She thought very highly of her, I can tell by the way she talks about Holly. Michelle got picked on a lot too when she was younger. Maybe that's why they were such good friends. Hey, what do you know about Jimmy Jendron?"

Holly's father groaned.

"Stay away from him, he's bad news!"

"In what way?"

"He's connected. That's all I'm going to say. He gets what he wants, when he wants it."

Holly's father hung up.

Sitting alone in the quiet house, Rick couldn't get the conversations with Holly's father and Jimmy Jendron out of his head.

Then he got an idea. He went out the door.

Rick stepped into The Periwinkle. He was wearing a disguise; a Stetson, and an old pair of glasses. After all, he and Michelle had eaten at The Periwinkle many times and someone would recognize him.

The bar section was quiet, with only two other customers sitting at a table. Nobody was at the bar, so he sat there and ordered a Rum and Coke.

"Wow, it's been a long time since I've been here!" said Rick. "But it's still pretty much like I remember it!"

The bartender, a graying man in his fifties put the drink down.

"When was the last time you were here?" he asked.

"Oh, let's see, oh yeah, it had to be '82!"

"Yeah, that *was* quite a while ago!"

"Yeah, I'll never forget that day. My friends and I were having burgers, right over by that window, and there's all this commotion! I guess some girl fell from the roof of the apartments next door!"

"Oh, yeah!" he said. "She landed on my cook's car! Demolished it! Brand new Corvette!"

"So what do you know about it? Was it suicide? Drugs? Was that building known for shady stuff . . ."

The bartender glared at Rick. Then he grabbed Rick by the wrist and twisted it.

"We don't talk about that around here!" he yelled. "Finish your drink and get out! I don't want any trouble! I know who you are! You've been here many times! Your disguise didn't fool me! Get out! NOW!"

Rick gulped the rest of the drink and threw his money on the bar.

Once Rick left, the bartender picked up the phone and dialed. He went in the corner and talked to someone in a hushed voice.

"That's right!" he said. "This guy was asking about her!"

Rick got to the door of Twilight Towers. He pulled a screwdriver-like device from his pocket and put it in the lock, shaking the tumblers until the lock gave way. Then he went inside.

Rick took the elevator to the fourth floor. He walked through the hall to get to the common balcony. There, at the first unit, was a barbecue grill. He looked at it, looked at the window of the condo, but noticed it was covered by a curtain.

He went to the balcony railing and looked down. A bus went by on the street below. Then he sized the width of the railing up with his hands. It was about 9 3/4" wide. He stood on it. Then he sat on it, facing the wall. Then he fell.

A van pulled up to The Periwinkle. Two men got out and went in.

They came out with the bartender. The bartender pointed to the fourth floor of Twilight Towers.

Rick fell forwards, landing on the deck. He did it on purpose.

Once he left the building, he walked along the railing by the water.

A white van pulled up to him. The side door opened, and someone pushed him into it from behind. Then they closed the door and the van sped away.

Two of Rick's captors wore president's masks. The driver wore an owl's mask with big eyes and a long beak. He never spoke.

There were three in all.

"Who are you guys?"

"SHUT UP!" yelled the bigger man, wearing a George Washington mask. "Open your mouth again, and I'll break every bone in your body!"

He could do it, too, Rick thought.

The van drove for what seemed like an eternity. It must've been at least two hours.

No one said another word the whole trip. Not the driver or anybody else.

Rick had his back to the windshield, and there were no other windows. He dared not move or turn around.

Then the van stopped.

"You've been asking too many questions," said a smaller man, who wore an Abraham Lincoln mask. He put something up to Rick's face. *It was a hand grenade.*

"Keep asking questions, and your wife's going to end up dead. Blown to pieces. Maybe you too."

"Get out! Now!" said the bigger man.

They opened the door, shoved Rick out, and sped off.

He looked at the rear license plate. Someone had covered it with a thick layer of mud.

Rick didn't know where he was, but it was not a pretty place. Abandoned apartment buildings lined the streets. In some cases, just the shell of the buildings remained. There were burned out buildings, boarded up buildings, buildings with broken windows, glass all over the sidewalks, and weeds growing through the cracks.

There were bodies of cars, stripped down to their rims, resting on cement blocks. Gang graffiti decorated random surfaces.

Rick walked to the end of the street and turned. He was the only white person. Most of the younger people he saw wore gang colors.

"Yo, Holmes, can you spare some bills?" asked a teenage male. Rick gave him some money and walked away.

Rick kept walking. Soon he came to a fork in the street where there was a park. Sitting on a bench, an elderly African American man eyed Rick

Rick didn't know which way to go. Finally, he took the street to the right of the fork.

"Only a punk would walk that way!" said the man, shaking his head.

Rick turned and walked to the left. "Thank you."

"You're welcome."

It took him a half hour to find out where he was, in a war zone neighborhood. He asked someone where the subway station was. Then he took three different subway trains and two different buses to get home.

Once there, Rick called Megan and told her about his abduction, Jimmy's threat, the incident with the bartender at The Periwinkle, and his conversation with Holly's father.

Megan paid a visit to Jimmy's construction site the next day. She showed him her badge necklace.

"Can we talk in private?" asked Megan.

They went behind a shed. Jimmy fidgeted and had trouble making eye contact with Megan.

"So, what do you want, Detective?"

"I heard you threatened someone yesterday."

Jimmy forced a nervous laugh. "Rick? We're friends! I was just kidding around! I didn't think he'd take it to heart!"

"Then Rick got kidnapped. And threatened again."

"Oh my God! That's terrible!"

"Just out of curiosity, where were you yesterday at 3 PM?"

Jimmy opened his mouth to speak, but no words came out. Finally, he said: "What has that got to do with me?"

"Did I say it did? I was just curious, that's all. If you don't remember, that's fine. But it seems a little suspicious."

Jimmy shrugged.

"What do you know about Holly O'Brien?"

He winced. Then he looked away. "She was my next door neighbor. She was a lot younger than me. That's all I really know."

"Do you ever go to Twilight Towers?"

"I've been trying to get their renovation jobs for years now . . ."

"That's not what I asked."

"Yeah, I've been there. Why?"

"No reason. I'd just be very careful there. That's all. And I'd be careful about threatening people too. And kidnapping, you know that's a federal offense. But we can't prove it."

After Megan left, Jimmy probably made another call.

Later that day, Dunn called Megan.

"Be very careful of that condo," he said.

"Why? What have you got?"

"It's owned by someone I've been trying to find for years. Real bad news. This situation is like a hand grenade waiting to go off. Be very careful."

SEVENTEEN

"Now you're going to remember the day she actually fell."

LATE that night, a white ice cream truck with a side serving window and no license plates rolled into town, with music playing on the chimes. A heavy-set, muscular man wearing a white uniform complete with a white hat with a black brim was the driver. He had curly brown hair and blue eyes with a sleepy, slanted, cowboy look to them. And he sported a mustache and goatee. The rest of his face was unshaven with razor stubble.

The ice cream truck drove all over town, unnoticed, for over an hour. Since it was after midnight, few people were on the streets.

The driver lit a cigarette. It was a Camel. One of his ex-girlfriends once told him he looked like the guy from the old Camel ads.

The ice cream truck stopped near Twilight Towers.

You guessed right. The ice cream man was Dunn.

He walked along the street near Twilight Towers, getting a feel for the place. *Then he witnessed something very disturbing.*
First, he heard screams coming from the building. The screams of a young girl.

Then a man and a woman brought a teenage girl out the front door. She had long, black hair. A veil covered her face.

The girl thrashed and convulsed, screaming, trying to get away. But they held her tight.

They brought her to a parked car.

They didn't see Dunn. He was standing by the truck smoking a cigarette.

The woman got in the back seat with the girl, holding her as the girl continued to thrash about and scream.

The man got in the driver's seat and the car sped away, with the girl still screaming.

Less than five minutes later, the car came back around the block and stopped. The man, woman, and teenage girl got out. The girl wasn't screaming anymore. In fact, she was arm-in-arm with the older woman and they talked and laughed! So did the man.

They went back in the building.

Later, Dunn found out what had happened.

The next morning Dunn met Megan, Rick, and Victor at the police station.

They went to the monitoring room, where a black and white video screen showed Michelle sitting at a table twitching her wrist. The others would look on while Dunn hypnotized her.

Dunn and Megan sat down with the file folders and she updated him on everything. He in turn told her everything he knew.

Dunn noticed Megan observing the size of his arms. He glanced at her. She smiled.

They moved closer together to read the files. He looked over at Megan. She looked at him. They held the gaze for several seconds.

Dunn entered the interrogation room.

"Hi, Michelle."

She had a blank, empty look to her eyes. "Please call me Shelly. That's what Holly used to call me."

She looked his uniform up and down.

"Why the uniform?" she asked.

Dunn shrugged. "Just to build rapport."

Michelle chuckled.

"Okay, Shelly. So, what's the problem? Why are we here?"

He stared into her eyes and she stared into his, fixed in a trance.

"Holly is dead!" she cried out. Tears ran down her cheek. "I pushed her off the railing! They thought she fell off! She thought she could fly after we took LSD! Nobody knew! I *pushed* her!"

"It's okay, Shelly," said Dunn. "Shelly, tell me about Holly."

She sniffed and sobbed, wiping the tears from her eyes.

"She was misunderstood. No one understood her. Most people didn't like her. I can't really explain it. She was usually friendly but not always. Feisty. She wasn't afraid to tell anybody off.

104

"Most of the guys just used her for sex. And she'd get drugs or a place to crash from the guys. She never really said what was bothering her. Holly was a closed book. She acted so cool, but she wasn't really happy. Maybe she just didn't know what she wanted. I don't know. It's hard to explain. You'd have to see her to really understand what she was like."

"How did you meet her?"

"At the park. She was all dressed in black, smoking. I asked her for a cigarette. She was older than me, but she stayed back. Truancy. Stuff like that. Then she was in my class at school.

"My other friend, who I knew since kindergarten, ditched me for the popular clique. That really hurt. I wasn't *cool enough* for her new friends.

"Holly and I weren't popular. But the popular girls didn't pick on me when Holly was around. They were afraid of her. Holly protected me.

"My family was falling apart. Dad was losing his business. Mom was clueless about life. My sister was getting into drugs. We were never close."

"So, you looked up to Holly, almost like a big sister?"

"Yeah. But she always called me 'Little Girl.' I hated that! She kept calling me 'Little Girl!' I was smoking, drinking, and guys were touching me! But she kept calling me Little Girl!"

Dunn lit a cigarette.

"What did you do when you hung out with Holly?"

"Mostly drink cheap wine. Sometimes we'd smoke pot. We did cocaine. One time we tried heroin. Speed. You name it. Then that day we took acid and Holly got killed."

"Did you get *all* your drugs from Holly?"

"Mostly. When we were partying and some of the guys came on too strong she'd stop them. I was weak. She wasn't afraid of guys."

"And she protected you a lot?"

"Yeah. I was pretty clumsy. I'd get hurt. Like one time I fell on a wooden plank near the pier. I couldn't move. Holly carried me home that day. Boy, was I crying! Another time I accidentally ran into her elbow. Stupid me. Stuff like that."

"But Shelly, if Holly was such a good friend, why did you push her off the balcony?"

Michelle had a chilling, angry look on her face. "I told you! Because she kept calling me *Little Girl*!"

She told Dunn more and more. All the times they hung out together. All the details. He felt like he knew Holly.

Dunn took a drag off his cigarette. "It sounds like she was *very* hard to figure out."

Michelle nodded.

"Okay Shelly. Before I hypnotize you, why did you keep this a secret for over twenty years? You could go to prison!"

Michelle sobbed and put her head down.

"The nightmares! I was seeing things! I went to her grave! And I went to that building every night! One night I heard screaming and I looked up to the fourth floor, and saw her! She was wearing a mask on one side of her face, looking down at me! I ran up the stairs, but nobody was there!"

Suddenly, Dunn remembered the girl with the veil.

"Then I broke a mirror in my bathroom! There was a mirror in the condo that day we took LSD! I had a flashback! I can't stop thinking about it! I saw a teenage girl walking near the water! I thought she was Holly! I even shook her up and called her Holly! The poor girl must've freaked out! She must've thought I was . . . crazy . . . I didn't even remember that! Megan told me!"

"Anything else?"

"At school one day, where I used to teach, I saw a girl that reminded me of Holly twist another girl's wrist. That's what Holly used to do to me! I pushed the girl into a wall!"

Dunn noticed that Michelle was twitching her wrist.

"Shelly, do you think it would help if we went back to the building where it happened, and I hypnotized you there?"

When Megan, Rick, Dunn, and Michelle got outside, Michelle noticed the ice cream truck.

"Let's go in that!" she said, pointing to it.

Dunn looked at Megan, who nodded her approval. They all piled into the truck and headed for Twilight Towers.

"Turn on the music!" said Michelle.

Dunn flicked a switch and the truck chimes started to play *Turkey In The Straw*.

Megan turned her two-way radio off so it wouldn't distract her.

Michelle sat on the floor near the dashboard, repeatedly pressing the button that rang the bell.

Keeping his eye on the rear view mirror, Dunn noticed that a white van was following them, three cars back. He didn't tell the others. But he pressed a red button on his phone.

"Why didn't Victor come with us?" asked Megan.

"He's doing something else," said Dunn. "You'll see later."

They arrived at Twilight Towers and went in the front door.

"Holly used to hang around with an older man who lived here," said Michelle. "He got her booze and drugs, and let teenagers hang around. I guess he was from a wealthy family. But he had a bad reputation."

They rode up in the elevator and got off on the fourth floor. Michelle led them through the hall to the front porch. She pointed to the porch railing of the condo on the end.

"That's the last place I saw Holly alive."

"Okay, Shelly," said Dunn. "Are you ready?"

Suddenly, Michelle's face turned pale.

"Megan, Rick, I'm scared!" she said. "Now I'm not sure if I want to remember this!"

Megan patted her on the shoulder.

"It's alright, Shelly," she said. "We're all here to help you."

Dunn grabbed her wrist and pulled, much like Holly had one day. "Shelly, you're going to remember when you and Holly took LSD at this condo. You're going to remember everything, exactly how it happened."

Michelle went into a trance.

"It was a day in early spring." Michelle said. *"The sun was shining brightly and it was ten o'clock in the morning."*

Michelle had played hooky. She went to meet Holly at the condo. They had planned it for almost a week.

"I kept pestering Holly to get me acid, so I could try it. Every day I would ask her. Finally, she did."

When she got to the front door, she pushed the button to ring the condo. There was no answer. So she rang another doorbell. Then she rang it again. Whoever it was buzzed her through the front door. She heard a baby crying in the background through the intercom.

She took the elevator up to the fourth floor. She had butterflies in her stomach. This would be a new experience for her. She had never tried LSD before. Holly would be there to help her.

Once on the fourth floor, on the balcony, she knocked on the door. No answer. So she sat on the railing to wait. Her skinny butt fit perfectly.

After what seemed like forever, Holly opened the door. She had bleached her hair again.

"Hi Little Girl!" she said. "Ready for your big trip?"

Michelle gritted her teeth. She had told Holly so many times not to call her that.

Michelle went in the condo and they sat down on the striped sofa. On the coffee table was a wrestling magazine. The cover pictured two sweaty wrestlers, one of whom had the other in a hold. The one in the hold had his mouth open, like he was screaming.

Also on the table was a Rubik's Cube. Michelle grabbed it and started to fiddle with it.

"I can solve that puzzle in like, two seconds," said Holly. She pulled out two small pieces of paper, each a little bigger than a postage stamp. They had yellow smiley faces ☺ on them.

Michelle was really nervous. This was it. Maybe Holly would stop calling her 'Little Girl.'

"Shelly, just lick the paper." Holly licked hers.

Michelle held her breath and licked the one in her hand.

Nothing happened at first.

"It'll take about twenty minutes to feel it," said Holly.

She got up and turned on the music. Oysters In A Sandbox *came through the speakers.*

"Want something to drink?" asked Holly. "Maybe a soda?"

Michelle shook her head. Holly had a mixed drink in her hand; Vodka and fruit juice.

It started in the stomach. Little butterflies. Fluttering. Fluttering some more. Then they were swarming in her stomach.

Suddenly, everything was coming at her at once; the music, the sunlight streaming in the window, and Holly's voice talking to her.

She turned to look at Holly, and Holly's eyes lit up like green lights on a Christmas tree. Holly was a monster. She changed into an alien, then back to Holly. Then back to an alien. She hissed. Then back into Holly.

108

Michelle stood up from the couch and suddenly realized she couldn't feel her legs. Actually, she couldn't feel any part of her body. So she laughed out loud. Her laugh echoed all over the condo, like the huge echo from the gym.

Then she caught herself staring at the wallpaper. It had this strange pattern. Then it turned into snakes! It was a whole mess of millions of snakes squirming on the wall!

The condo turned into a space station and they were flying through space. Holly was the commando. Uncle Owl, with his big eyes and beak, was the captain.

Then the window overlooking the water flew open for no reason. It scared them so much that they both ran and hid behind the sofa.

"What was that?" screamed Michelle.

"I don't know!" said Holly.

Michelle felt her forearm. There were millions of spiders crawling under her skin.

"No!" she screamed, scratching, trying to get them off.

"Shelly! It's alright!"

She held Michelle's wrist and twisted it.

"You can't tell anyone!" she said. "Keep your cool!"

A green Volkswagen bug with no wheels and bright headlight eyes floated around the room, angry at Michelle, staring at her. If she got too close it would sting her and make her disappear.

Blue and green peacock flowers lighted up and flew around. The Indian mask on the wall with long black hair and big eyes lighted up and spun around.

Everything was happening one after the other, there was no down time.

The screaming wrestler on the magazine cover actually screamed out loud. Michelle could hear the color of his voice; it was deep, ocean blue.

The wrestler holding him was hot. He tasted like a fine piece of prime rib. Michelle wanted him on top of her.

She heard the sound of a vacuum cleaner. It was coming from the next condo.

A thought struck Michelle. If she were to go outside, and look in the window, she would see herself on the living room floor of the condo. And another Michelle could look in another window, and see Michelle looking in a window, looking at a Michelle on the floor, *and then another Michelle could look in another window, and see two Michelles looking in two identical windows, looking at Michelle on the living room floor of the condo and another Michelle could look in another window and see three Michelles looking in three identical windows . . ."*

All the colors on the Rubik's Cube had certain meaning. Imagine if you had a tile floor just like the Rubik's Cube? That would be wild! The colors of the cube started to make sounds. They sounded like a heavenly choir buried in special effects.

Klarngy Jarng! (Some man's name that was also a sound. It was shaped like a hexagon.)

Wow. Michelle found herself running to the door. She went onto the balcony, where she heard the vacuum cleaner even louder. And a little baby boy was staring at them through the glass on the door of the next condo.

"Shelly, I can fly!" said Holly. She got up on the balcony railing.

"No you can't!" said Michelle.

"Yes I can! Come fly with me, Little Girl!"

"Holly! Be careful! We're on the fourth floor!"

Michelle looked over the railing. Cars were whizzing by on the street below. She saw a row of green trees, and they all turned into green monsters with antennas and huge yellow eyes, holding each other and making out.

Rows of mystical sunflowers came to life and danced around below.

Holly flapped her arms.

"Holly, come down from there!"

"No, you come up!"

Holly leaned forward and lost her balance. One foot went off the edge. She teetered forward.

Michelle tried to grab her arm, but it was too late.

In an instant, Holly got her balance back and fell backwards, landing on the deck.

They both went back into the condo.

The music was loud and it was making all kinds of pretty colors and shapes.

The voice sang: "Oysters in a sandbox, that is what we are . . ."

Michelle turned and saw herself. It was a mirror. She screamed. It was the most hideous face she had ever seen in her life!

110

Wait! It wasn't a mirror! It was the Indian mask! She was face-to-face with it! Where was the real mirror?

She found it. Then she screamed again. There was two of her! She didn't want there to be two of her! Because then someone would look in a mirror and see her, and she would look in a mirror and see another girl just like her looking in a mirror, and that girl would be looking in a mirror, seeing another girl just like her looking in a mirror. So there would be a million of her! And how would she know which one she was?

Michelle punched the mirror and it shattered onto the floor. She could hear the pieces, and see the colors they made, and taste them, and they tasted like sugar cubes.

Holly was gone. Gone.

Michelle ran back onto the porch and looked over the railing. There was Holly on the sidewalk below, face down.

"No!" screamed Michelle. "She wasn't lying on the sidewalk! That was when she fell down in the gym! I got the two times mixed up!"

Michelle went back in the condo.

There were two Victorian dolls on a shelf. Their eyes were real! Oh my God! They used to be real people, but someone made them into dolls! What if someone made Michelle into a doll? And she couldn't move?

She felt her heart beating. It could stop at any moment, she thought.

Then Michelle had the most terrifying thought of all. She didn't know what was going to happen next. *That thought scared her like nothing else.*

Then there was a man. He was really a skeleton. He kept turning into a skeleton. Then he kept turning back into a man.

He was short and thin with white hair and a white moustache.

He was talking to Michelle, and she was talking to him, but she wasn't aware of what they were really saying.

Words made out of rubber. Bouncing all over the room.

He sat her on the couch. Then he kissed her, licked her neck, and touched her chest. Then he tried to take her shirt off.

"No!" screamed Michelle.

Michelle looked at the walls and gasped. They were all eyes! Millions of eyes were on the wall staring at her!

111

"Stop!" she yelled. "Don't look at me! Stop staring!"

She looked at the man. "Stop!" she yelled. "I'm only fourteen!"

There was a statue of an angel on the entertainment center. When Michelle stared at it, it flew around the room.

"Holly, stop flying around the room!"

"The days we had were ours/But we had too much fun/The chances that we took/were all 'cause we were young/The moon turned to sun/The stars you're among."

Then Holly came in. She was a hissing serpent woman, but she changed back to Holly. When she saw what was happening, she started to cry.

Holly had a skull in her hand – no, it was actually a shoe. One of her shoes with the red hearts on the bottom.

"Aaaah!" The man screamed.

Holly hit the man in the head with the shoe. Then she hit him again.

The man got off Michelle. She started to crawl towards the door.

But then there were eight men in the room. Actually, they were soldiers from the galaxy of the conquering space ship. Their eyes and teeth were bright lights. All of their faces were distorted; shaped like triangles, mushrooms, or hour glasses; too long, too short, the eyes too close together, or the eyes too far apart. One wore a Mardi gras mask with long feathers sticking up. Another wore a mole costume with no eyes and big teeth.

They all grabbed Holly and took her into the bedroom and closed the door. She screamed and tried to fight them.

Michelle listened, and Holly was crying. She was screaming and crying loud like the day she fell down in the gym.

Michelle banged on the door. The door was locked.

"Leave her alone!" she yelled. "I'll call the police!"

"I live here!" yelled the voice of the man who had been fondling her. "I'll have you arrested for cutting school, doing drugs, and trespassing! They'll send you to DYS 'til you're twenty-one! Nobody will believe you anyway! Do you know who my family is?"

"Oysters in a sandbox/That is what you are/Oysters in a sandbox hid from life/Oysters in a sandbox may grow old/But they never die/There once was a time/When I was bad to you/There once was a time/When you were there for me/I fell from grace/You slipped away . . ."

Michelle ran out to the balcony and got up on the railing.
She had to do this. She had to. It would be over in a minute. She couldn't.

"No! Let me go!" screamed Michelle.

Rick, Megan, and Dunn held her down on the deck until she calmed down.

When Megan stood up, she noticed a drop of something on the railing. She could tell it had been there for a long time. It was a drop of blood. She could tell by the color. Human blood. She knew it from her crime scene training. Then it dawned on her. *It might be Michelle's blood from over twenty years ago.*

Michelle realized where she was. They took her back into the condo.

The condo had the exact same furniture she remembered. Also, the Rubik's Cube and the wrestling magazine were there. Just the way it looked back in 1982.

Michelle was trembling, sweat pouring down her forehead.

"Then what'd you do, Shelly?" asked Dunn.

Michelle was back in time again. The building was suspended in the air, and the area beyond the balcony was a painting, so you couldn't get hurt even if you fell from there. Everything was made of liquid. You could walk through walls.

Michelle heard screeching electric guitars in her mind. Or it may have been someone actually playing the guitar in another condo. Every color made a sound. She could taste shapes. A square tasted like a graham cracker. A circle was like a church wafer.

A pretty ballerina danced across the sky.

Holly was in there with the men. The space men. They were going to tele-transport her to another space ship.

Michelle looked to the door of the next condo. The little baby boy was in the window again. Michelle saw his future in a split second. He would be a nice kid, too nice, picked on, like her, but he could never go back to being a little boy.

The vacuum cleaner was going, and that sound tasted like blue metal air.

Then a man came to the window of the door of the next condo. He picked up the baby boy. She knew that man now, it was – no it couldn't be – it was – no it couldn't be – MR. KINECKI!

"MR. KINECKI!" Michelle screamed out loud.

And there he was, in the room with them, accompanied by Victor.

"Michelle," said Mr. Kinecki, "I didn't know that was you! I was the one who buzzed you in that day! You kept ringing our doorbell! I didn't know that girl who fell was your friend!"

He sank into a living room chair.

"Tell her what happened," said Dunn. "You see, I looked up the history of everybody who ever lived here. I found it ironic that not only was Mr. Kinecki Michelle's boss, but he also lived in the building Holly fell from."

Mr. Kinecki sighed. "Well, about twenty years ago, we rented a condo here, next door. The rents were fairly reasonable back then, and I wasn't making much at my teaching job in Burlington, and we had a young family . . . we didn't live here long . . ." he shook his head. "Too many strange things happening, and drugs . . . late night parties . . . beer cans left in the halls . . . needles . . . pipes . . . anyway, my little son Billy was sick, so I called in sick that day myself. My wife wanted me home. When Billy got up, he went to the door window, pointing. We had heard a lot of loud music and commotion all morning. People yelling and screaming. We didn't call the police because once you start telling on people . . . well . . . you know what happens. Especially when there're drugs involved. I saw two girls near the railing. Your friend was standing on it! But you pulled her back down, or she went back down, or something. I couldn't hear what you were saying because my wife had the vacuum cleaner going . . ."

Michelle's mouth fell open. "I pushed her another time! I know I did!"

"Let's go back to that other time," said Dunn.

Victor led Mr. Kinecki out the door.

Dunn grabbed Michelle's wrist and pulled. She went into her trance again.

Michelle was outside the condo, on the porch. Colors and shapes swirled everywhere and noises filled the air. The cries of seagulls, the cars on the street, voices, and men working on a roof nearby, (who turned into gorillas when Michelle looked at them), all formed one big symphony of sound.

Michelle just wanted to turn it off. "Stop the world I want to get off!" How long would it take to come down from acid? Four hours? Maybe eight?

Holly was in there with those men and she was crying. Michelle tried to go back in the condo. The door was locked. She knocked on the door. No answer. She knocked again.

"Go away!" someone yelled.

"I'm going to call the police if you don't let her go!" she yelled, breaking into tears.

"Go ahead!"

Michelle hit the storm door so hard that it shattered all over the deck. Pieces went everywhere and her hand was cut. But she didn't feel it.

She ran through the hall door and flew down all flights of stairs to the street below.

There were people on the streets. One man, wearing mirrored glasses, was really a spy from The Soviet Union. His watch was a radio and he wanted to kill Michelle because she was an American.

There could be nuclear war anytime. A mushroom cloud like the shape of the guy's head up in the condo.

Then there were people walking near the restaurant. Their eyes glowed and they kept turning into cartoon characters with big eyes, then back into people. They were the cartoon people. Michelle knew they wanted to kill her. So she ran to the beach. On the way, she noticed that all the telephone poles were bent and twisted.

A big machine that made noise in a field wanted to suck her up. It was invisible and sounded like an organ.

She tripped over a rock and fell. When she stood up, her knees were bleeding through her pants. The blood sounded like a harpsichord, but Michelle couldn't feel any pain.

Then there was a feeling of overwhelming joy, like everything was going to be alright. Michelle was in heaven.

Headlights everywhere! Surrounding her. Following her! No! They were really eyes!

There was an octopus man with a beard and millions of legs and scales. He wore a stocking cap. Part human, part aqua life. He came from a hole in the bottom of the sea.

Then, suddenly, she saw the future. Holly was going to die. She didn't know how, but she knew it was going to happen.

It was as though Michelle could see years into the future, even Rick. She understood everything now. She found the secret to life –

to be happy. The most important thing about life is people, she thought.

Still with no feeling in her body, Michelle ran back to the building and got in the front door somehow. She ran up to the fourth floor.

There was Holly, sitting on the balcony railing, crying. Her black leotard was ripped.

Michelle didn't know what to say to her. They just stared at each other.

Music was flowing out of the condo. Oysters In A Sandbox.

"Holly, what did those guys do to you?"

She sobbed. "What do you think they did, Little Girl?"

No. They wouldn't. They didn't. Holly didn't. Eight guys, one after the other? Or all at once?

" . . . I . . . tried . . . to stop them . . ." Michelle stammered.

"I know. You couldn't. Nobody could. You got away. Little Girl got away. They wanted you. That was the deal. Acid and booze for you. Then if they got in trouble they could say you were on drugs. Nobody would believe you. But I couldn't let them do that to you, Little Girl. And that acid might've been laced with PCP – Angel Dust!"

Michelle's rage overwhelmed her.

"YOU SET ME UP! YOU CALL ME 'LITTLE GIRL', THEN YOU MAKE A DRUG DEAL WHERE I HAVE TO DO EIGHT GUYS! WITH ANGEL DUST!"

It took Michelle by surprise. It was like she had left her body. Someone else was in her body controlling it, not her.

She ran at Holly and punched her repeatedly, as hard as she could. Left and right. In the face. On the arms. In the stomach. On the boobs. On the love handles.

Holly laughed hysterically and pushed Michelle back. Michelle kept punching.

Since Michelle was weak, her punches had no effect. They just made Holly laugh harder.

Michelle made a feeble effort to push Holly. Holly started to fall backwards.

Holly looked Michelle in the eyes. Holly looked hurt. Michelle tried to grab Holly before she fell. But Holly got her balance back. She laughed even louder.

116

Michelle grabbed Holly's hair. Holly put both her hands on Michelle's wrist and twisted. Michelle let go. So did Holly.

Michelle started to walk away. She got to the door leading to the stairs – several feet away.

Then it happened. Holly was laughing so hard, she leaned back and fell off the railing. Holly's feet went over the railing; Michelle saw the red hearts on the soles of Holly's shoes.

Holly screamed a pathetic, lonely cry, like a seagull flying out to sea.

Michelle held her breath, waiting for the inevitable. A whole century passed before Holly hit the ground.

There was the crash. It sounded like a train hitting a car. Michelle shuddered. She backed up against the wall and sank to the deck. She wanted to throw up.

No. That didn't just happen. It couldn't have happened.

"Call an ambulance!" someone yelled four floors down.

So Michelle hid under the stairway and snuck out once it got dark.

Silence.

Michelle fought to catch her breath.

"I've got some questions for you, Shelly," said Dunn.

"What color was Holly's hair that day?"

"Blonde. She bleached it blonde."

Dunn looked in a folder. "But it says here she had light brown hair when they found her."

"Oh yeah, maybe it was."

"Or was it black? Or was it auburn?"

Michelle thought about it. "Yes! That was it! It was black! I saw her in the coffin! She had black hair!"

Dunn shook his head. "No. She had light brown hair. Her family wanted her hair dyed black for the funeral. Her natural color was actually auburn. It's all right here. And she didn't fall the day you guys took acid."

"YES SHE DID!"

"I've got a surprise for you, Shelly," said Dunn. "VICTOR!"

Mr. Kinecki came in the door again, followed by Victor.

"Michelle, Holly fell over a week later, and you weren't even here!" said Mr. Kinecki. "Little Billy ran and got me when he saw her fall off the railing. He saw it through the door. He was still learning to talk, but he kept saying: 'Daddy, girly fall! Boo-boo! Daddy, girly fall! UH-OH!'"

Silence.

Megan's eyes filled with tears. "Billy saw it happen? But why didn't you tell the police?"

Mr. Kinecki looked away. "With the type of people who lived in this building at the time, and having a young family, I thought it better not to get involved. Besides, they never asked me. When the emergency crews came I took the kids and left."

"Mr. Kinecki," said Megan. "Was anybody else on the balcony with Holly, or was she all alone?"

"I don't think anybody else was there. At least I didn't hear anybody. And Billy never mentioned another person. Of course, he was pretty small at the time . . ."

Dunn grabbed Michelle by the wrist again. "Now you're going to remember the day she actually fell."

EIGHTEEN

"Victor, what's wrong?"

DUNN grabbed Michelle by the wrist again. "Now you're going to remember the day she actually fell."

"NO!" screamed Michelle. "No! Don't make me remember! I can't remember! It's too much! I don't want to see Holly die again!"

"Shelly, the only way you'll ever be free is if you remember the truth." Dunn said. "We have to get to the truth. They never got to the truth about my dad, and he died. Holly can't speak anymore. You have to speak for her. She wants you to! You *owe* her that for all the times she saved you!"

Michelle went back in time to that day. *It was a typical spring day; sunny, breezy,, and not too hot. She hadn't seen Holly much all week. After the acid trip, she vowed to cut down on drugs. Certainly no more acid. Cocaine and heroin were also out. She would smoke weed once in a while, and maybe have a few drinks at a party. That was it.*

She would see Holly at school and they would hang around during the day. But she was ducking Holly outside of school, and had turned down a few offers from Holly that week to get together and party.

On a Monday afternoon, Holly called Michelle. Michelle was starting to miss Holly, and could tell by the strain in Holly's voice that she was afraid Michelle didn't want to hang out with her anymore. Finally, Michelle agreed to meet Holly at Twilight Towers.

"But Holly, how can you go there, after what they did to you that day?"

"Dave (the guy who owned the condo) didn't do it! It was his friends! He doesn't want them around anymore! And I'm living there now! My dad threw me out of the house! And Dave won't be there anyway – I promise."

Michelle sighed. "And Holly needed her drugs and alcohol too – she always got them at the condo!

"I planned on hanging around with Holly all summer. Boy, were we going to have fun! But I planned on having a talk with her about drugs, and how I wanted to cut down. No more hard stuff. Holly would understand."

An hour before she was to meet Holly there, Michelle and her mother had a major blowout concerning Michelle's slipping grades, trouble at school, the type of company she was keeping, and the places she was hanging around.

"We yelled and screamed at each other for over an hour," said Michelle, "And then we both cried. I called her a ditsy, clueless, white-bread suburban housewife."

Suddenly, Michelle realized that the argument with her mother had already made her a half hour late for meeting Holly. She ran out the door.

On the way, three police cars passed her, sirens blaring, blue lights flashing. Then a fire engine and an ambulance passed by.

Michelle fell on the floor, writhing.

"NO! I CAN'T REMEMBER! STOP!"

"Stop!" yelled Rick. "Look what it's doing to her! You're going to kill her!"

Rick ran over to Dunn and shoved him hard.

"She's almost there!" yelled Dunn. "Sometimes you feel the most pain right before you get better! And if you ever put your hands on me again, you'll spend the rest of your life in a wheelchair!"

Dunn sat down on the floor with her and pulled her wrist again. "Okay, Shelly, you saw the ambulance go by. Then what happened?"

Michelle struggled to speak. ". . . when . . . I . . . got . . . to Twilight . . . Towers, the street was blocked off and a crowd had gathered. There was a parked car with the windshield smashed and the roof caved in. I remember now. It was a Corvette."

They put the stretcher in the ambulance just as she got there. The person in the ambulance was only wearing one shoe. It had red hearts on the sole. It was Holly.

In the street, next to the smashed Corvette, Michelle saw another shoe. It too had hearts on the sole.

The ambulance sped off.

Michelle came out of her trance. It was as if Michelle had seen a video of the whole thing, but still didn't believe it.

"NO! I PUSHED HER OFF! I KNOW I PUSHED HER OFF!"

"No you didn't, Shelly!" said Megan.

"You felt guilty," said Rick. "You felt so terrible about what happened to her, your mind made you think you did it. And you had a plausible story if you were accused of it; that Holly thought she could fly after taking LSD!"

"NO!" screamed Michelle.

"Shelly, what was the weather like the day you pushed Holly?" asked Dunn.

Michelle thought about it. "It was sunny! Like I said before – no! It was cloudy and rainy! Yeah! I remember now!"

Dunn picked up a folder. "National Weather service report for May 17, 1982, 6 PM. Sunny, 0 precipitation, high 69 low 53."

Michelle stared at the wall.

"If you pushed Holly, you would've remembered the weather!" said Megan.

Silence.

Michelle looked at everybody. Her face turned red and tears rolled down her cheeks.

Rick tried to console her, but she stood up.

"NO! OH MY GOD! NO! I COULDN'T SAVE HER! She saved me so many times! But I couldn't save her *once*! She was my friend! I don't care what anybody else says about her! She was my *friend*! I loved her! She *needed* me! I needed *her*! She died all alone! She was always there for me! But she died all alone!"

Michelle ran over to a mirror hanging on the wall. She grabbed it and threw it on the floor. Pieces of glass went everywhere.

"I was supposed to be there! Nobody cared about her! I was late so she probably didn't think I was coming! She must've been so sad!

"It was a stupid accident! Just a *stupid* accident! It wasn't supposed to end like that! I never got to say 'Goodbye!' IT WASN'T FAIR! We were going to have fun all summer . . . IT WASN'T SUPPOSED TO HAPPEN! If I were there, it wouldn't have . . ."

She put her head down and sobbed, gasping for breath.

Then Michelle glared at Dunn.

"You bastard! I hate you! I hate you for making me remember that!"

"I'd rather have you hate me a little right now than have you spend the rest of your life as a prisoner of your own mind. I hated that my father got killed, but hated the fact that they never found the truth even more . . ."

Then an idea struck Dunn. "There's one more possibility," he said. "Just to explore all possibilities . . . was Holly suicidal? Would she have jumped on purpose?"

"NO!" screamed Michelle.

"Remember," said Megan, "that witness who saw her lean back and fall? Holly may have been on drugs or drinking, but the witness saw her lean back and fall!"

Dunn kept toying with the thought. "She could've made it *look* like an accident . . ."

"But this building isn't high enough to guarantee death from a fall," said Rick. "I mean, you could end up just being a vegetable for the rest of your life. I would think a suicide attempt would need something higher or more certain."

"Well," said Dunn, "desperate people do desperate things. Everybody in law enforcement has seen some crazy things happen, but I guess you're right. In this case suicide is speculation. There really isn't enough proof to say it happened like that."

"Holly wouldn't do it. I know that," said Michelle.

"Even after being worked by eight guys?" asked Dunn.

"That wouldn't bother Holly like it would bother someone else."

"There's another possibility," he said. "Those guys who assaulted Holly might've been afraid she'd tell on them. I wonder if *they* made it look like an accident . . ."

"But the witness!" said Megan.

"I know." Dunn said. "We know her name, but who was she? Obviously, we can't ask her about it because she's dead. But I wonder if she had any connection to those men – and the guy who lived here."

"Who knows?" said Rick.

"Shelly," said Dunn, "what do you know about the guy who lived here?"

"I only met him once - he came on to me, he chased teenage girls, he got Holly drugs . . . and he was from a wealthy family!"

"A *very* wealthy family!" said Dunn. "A major retail company that's traded on Wall Street! If I said the name, you'd know it!"

"Which one?" asked Rick.

"I'm not at liberty to say. I'm still working on a case. But the guy who lived here used the name David Coda. We call him "Little Davey Coda." He's been trafficking drugs for years! And weapons! Hand grenades, guns, cocaine, heroin, you name it! This condo was what you might call a retail drug and weapons boutique!"

"Oh my God!" cried Megan.

Suddenly, sirens filled the air. Then there was a commotion below. Voices yelled: "Step out of the vehicle! Get on the ground! Now!"

Dogs barking. More sirens.

Megan went out to the porch, and then came running back in.

"Oh my God!" she yelled. "There's like five marked cars down there! The officers have dogs and everything! The ATF is here! And they're arresting some guys in a white van! They're bringing them in the building!"

"That's what Victor was working on," said Dunn. "He went to get Mr. Kinecki, who I talked to last night. On the way here, I saw a white van following us and watching the building. I need for you to take a look at them. I think they might be some of the guys who attacked Holly."

Dunn opened his cell phone radio. "Bring 'em in now!" he said.

Victor and four uniformed officers brought in two men. The men were in handcuffs.

The first man had long, thick, feathered hair, a stringy, rat-haired moustache, and a huge pair of glasses that covered almost his whole face. The other man was tall, had wavy black hair, and pock-marks on the left side of his face.

Michelle stared at them. Rick's mouth fell open.

"Jimmy! Jimmy Jendron!" he yelled. He realized he had talked about Jimmy over the years, but Michelle had never met him.

Jimmy started to cry.

"No wonder why you got so upset when I asked you about Holly!" Rick said.

Victor hung his head low, with tears in his eyes.

"Victor, what's wrong?" asked Megan.

"You'll see in a minute," said Dunn.

More uniformed officers brought in two more men. One of the men was in his fifties and graying. The other was short and thin with a slight moustache.

"SERGEANT ANTONELLI!" screamed Megan.

Victor broke down in tears. He looked at Sergeant Antonelli.

"You scumbag!" he yelled. "You trained me! I looked up to you! Then what did you do, you cover up a drugs and weapons operation and abuse a young girl!"

Victor went over and punched him in the face. Antonelli fell to his knees.

Rick pointed to the graying man. "He's the bartender at The Periwinkle! He threw me out! He must have told his buddies I was asking about Holly!"

Michelle kept staring at the men.

"You creeps!" she yelled. "I'll never forget those creeps! They took Holly in the bedroom! YOU FUCKIN' AMINALS!"

She ran at them and started punching the man with the glasses, knocking them off his face. He cowered away. She spat on him and kicked him in the groin.

Rick, Dunn, and Megan tried to hold her as she thrashed around. The uniformed officers pushed the two men out the door.

"You gutless perverts!" screamed Michelle. "It took eight of you! You had to use drugs to get little girls 'cause you're so disgusting nobody wants you!"

Jimmy wailed from behind the door, sobbing. "I didn't touch that girl! I swear on my mother's urn! I tried to stop them! They had me by the balls . . . and they knew it!"

"What he means," said Dunn, "is that he was one of Little Davey's key men. He ran the show for Little Davey, so Little Davey wouldn't get caught. He couldn't rat on them or they'd take him down too. But now he can. He cleaned himself up. And if he helps us nail the other four, he'll get a lighter sentence."

"I will," said Jimmy. "I will."

The officers took him away.

"Obviously, Sergeant Antonelli is another one of Davey's men." Dunn said. "Little Davey still owns this place. We're still looking for him. We'll find him one of these days."

Michelle looked at her wrist. So did everybody else. She wasn't twitching it anymore.

"My wrist . . ."

". . . was what Holly used to anchor and trigger you into not telling on her, or yourself," said Megan. "You weren't consciously aware of it, and Holly probably didn't even do it on purpose! So when you didn't want people to find out about Holly, or what had happened, your wrist twitched, unconsciously, to remind you not to talk about it or to keep Holly's memory safe."

"So I used your wrist to hypnotize you!" said Dunn.

"Wow!" said Michelle. "I really thought I pushed her! I actually did, when we fought, but she didn't go over! But I really thought I pushed her off! I remember seeing her feet going over!"

"Your mind created that." said Megan. "You felt so guilty and sad about how it happened. It was like a computer trying to process too much information – it just shut off."

"You've been under a lot of pressure," said Rick. "Dealing with all those memories . . ."

"That stress built up," said Megan. "And then certain events and people made you think of what happened, and how bad you felt. *Oysters In A Sandbox* came at your most emotional peak, when Little Davey Coda was coming on to you."

"Anybody would've fallen apart," said Rick. "Your mind started playing tricks on you."

"And all your emotions about Holly came out too," said Megan. "You had a passionate relationship with her. What I mean by that is that there were times when you loved her, and times when you hated her. It was a constant struggle. All your emotions were tangled up. So when Ashley was picking on Sarah, it was Holly picking on you all over again. And when Ashley twisted Sarah's wrist – overload! It was Holly all over again, only now you had a job to protect other kids."

"The only way you could cope with Holly's death was by believing you pushed her off. Nothing is more dangerous than the human mind," said Dunn.

"I think Holly may have been abused before that day you took LSD," said Megan. "Promiscuity is a sign of that sometimes."

"Just so that I completely understand," said Victor, "Holly really did fall by accident? Little Davey's men had nothing to do with it?"

Dunn shrugged. "As far as we know. We'll have to believe what that witness said, unless we can prove she's connected to Little Davey Coda somehow. But I doubt she is. I found no information on her."

"Probably not," said Megan. "Too hard to pull off. Besides, Mr. Kinecki didn't say anything about a commotion before Holly fell. Billy saw her fall. If a bunch of guys threw her off there would've been more of a struggle."

Rick stared into space. "I'll never forget that terrible mescaline trip I took when I was sixteen. It happened two nights before Holly fell. When my grandmother asked me about a girl falling from Twilight Towers, I had this overwhelming feeling of Déjà vu. Then when I read about it in the paper, it was like I knew over twenty years ago that this whole thing would affect me somehow. It was like I could see into the future! The strangest feeling I ever had!"

Michelle hugged him. "Like you said, Holly was the wake up call. You didn't even know her, but she might've saved your life!"

Michelle looked at Megan. "Thank you, Megan. Thank you for everything you did. Thank you for not giving up on me and finding out the truth."

Megan smiled. "No problem! I just can't get over how little Billy Kinecki was here in this building that day! He broke the case for us! He's not even alive now, and yet *he* was one of the biggest clues! I never imagined in my police career that I would ever have to convince someone she *didn't* commit murder!"

"I want to quit the police department and work with Dunn!"

"I'd be glad to have you! And I pay a lot more than your lousy department does!"

Dunn put his arm around her. She put her arm around him.

Rick looked around the room. "How could you get to use this condo today?"

126

Dunn took out a cigarette, which Megan looked at disapprovingly. So he put it away.

"We made a deal with the guy who rents it from Little Davey. He sends his rent check to the family's Swiss trust fund. Anyway, what would Little Davey do if he found out we broke in and used it? Call the police?"

Everybody laughed.

"I can't believe I heard screams coming from this building," said Michelle. "I must've been really gone. I thought I saw Holly too . . ."

"I can explain that," said Dunn. "Her name is Victoria and she has a rare disease, similar to Epilepsy. Damn. I forget the name of it. Anyway, she wears a veil sometimes; it helps with the attacks. She can't stop screaming. Poor thing. But she seems to only get her attacks at night. I talked to her parents. The one thing that calms her down is taking her for a ride in the car."

"Poor kid!" said Victor.

"Yeah," said Dunn. "Her parents are trying to help her, but she spends a lot of time just staring out the window of their apartment on the end of this floor."

"That's what that was!" said Megan. "I've heard her scream too! But I could never figure out where the screams were coming from!"

Suddenly, a man came into the condo. He was short and thin, with a white moustache and long white hair, tied into a ponytail, flowing from the sides and back of his otherwise bald head.

He had something in his hand -- a Colt 45 with a silencer. He pointed the gun at them.

"Well, well, well, if it isn't Little Davey Coda!" said Dunn. "It's so nice to finally meet you!"

The white haired man clicked the safety latch off. "Too bad you won't live long enough to really get to know me! Sometimes it's better to leave the past alone! After all, Holly just fell by accident! Now you're all going to have to die!"

"Is it worth it?" said Megan. "Spending the rest of your life in prison?"

Little Davey laughed. "First of all, your cop buddies aren't here now! Second, my pilot's waiting with my chopper right outside! By the time they find your bodies, I'll be in some tropical country that has no extradition agreement with the United States! Do you know who my family is? We have property all over the world! And enough money to live anywhere! I'm not going to jail . . ."

Dunn lunged at him. Little Davey pulled the trigger. The bullet sliced into Dunn's chest; he fell to the floor.

Victor grabbed Little Davey's hands and pushed them upward. The gun went off again, the bullet hitting the ceiling.

Little Davey kicked Victor in the chest, knocking him back. Then he fired. The bullet grazed Victor's shoulder, sending him to floor.

While this was happening, Megan got behind Little Davey and locked her left arm under and around Little Davey's arm, and her right arm around his chin. Then she locked her hands together and tripped him to the floor. She held him down tightly.

"LET GO OF THE GUN RIGHT NOW OR I'LL BREAK YOUR NECK!" She yelled. "DO IT NOW!"

She applied pressure.

"OW!"

He let go of the gun. Rick ran over and kicked it out of his reach.

Megan handcuffed Little Davey.

Victor winced in pain, holding his shoulder. He crawled over to where Dunn lay.

"I think he's going to be alright!" said Victor. "He's wearing a bullet-proof vest!"

Dunn groaned. Victor helped him sit up.

". . . that was like getting hit by a tractor trailer . . ." Dunn gasped.

Two days later, the following story appeared in the paper:

Five Arrested On Drugs, Weapons, Attempted Murder Charges

Five men were arrested Monday morning and face either multiple drug, weapon, or attempted murder charges. John Antonelli, 60, James Jendron, 45, Brad Osgood, 55, Nelson Henry, 53, and David Coda, 63, all pleaded 'Not Guilty' at their arraignment yesterday.
ARREST continued on p. 129

ARREST (Continued from p. 128)

All were denied bail as they were considered a ". . . flight risk, and a danger to the community," by Assistant District Attorney Jennifer Kelley. All are due back in court on June 12.

Following a tip from an unidentified motorist who said a white van was involved in a road rage incident, police located and stopped the vehicle. When the driver reached for the paperwork, the officers noticed a hand grenade on the floor of the van. They called for backup immediately, and four of the men were detained at gunpoint while officers conducted a search. K-9 units and the Bureau of Alcohol, Tobacco, and Firearms were also called in.

The search revealed more weapons and explosives, including several assault rifles, handguns, bomb-making materials, and "Several hundred packets of white powder believed to be cocaine," police say.

Half an hour later, David Coda was arrested after he shot Sergeant Victor Gutierrez and another man during a scuffle at a nearby condominium development, Twilight Towers. Both victims suffered minor injuries and were treated and released.

Police say the two incidents are connected, and are still under investigation.

If convicted, the men face anywhere from five to twenty-five years in prison.

Not many people know what happened that night. After getting out of the hospital, Victor and Dunn took Little Davey Coda to a back room at the police station. They threw hot coffee in his face and boxed his ears. Then Dunn hit him with a bowling pin and flogged him with the sharp edge of a rolled up newspaper club. But he still didn't talk.

The next morning, Megan and Victor talked about what usually happens to a cop when he goes to prison. That night, Victor said a prayer for Sergeant Antonelli.

EPILOGUE

THE bulldozers came in. The workmen used explosives. They knocked The Caves down and took the pieces away in dump trucks.

Years later, there was a fire at Twilight Towers. A barbecue grill, left unattended, sprung a leak in the gas line and the top porch caught on fire. The fire destroyed the balcony railing before firefighters brought it under control.

Michelle spent many, many hours in therapy. She's doing well.

She started teaching again, at a small college. Her subject: *How To Start Your Own Business*. She uses her ice cream cart as an example and treats her students to ice cream.

One day, Megan and Dunn were drinking wine on the parapet to the castle in Denmark they had rented for the summer. They gazed out over the green hills and mist.

Kit Kat lay stretched out, licking his paws.

"I got another email from Victor," said Megan. "He needs some information on a suspect in a case. I'll get it to him tonight. I'm so glad he got promoted. Captain Gutierrez has such a nice ring to it. I'll bet he'll be Chief someday."

"Don't forget to remind our contacts about those other three guys we're after. The ones who abused Holly and Michelle in Little Davey's condo. That Jimmy Jendron guy was a big help. We need to make sure we protect him."

"What's going to happen to those three other guys?"

"They'll just disappear in a plane if they don't make amends. That's all."

Megan shook her head. "I'll never get over that case. Imagine what was going through Michelle's mind?"

"That was an amazing case. And you were the one who took Little Davey down! After all the years I spent trying to catch him, it was you! I can't believe it! And you got me to quit smoking!"

Later, Michelle and Rick went to the cemetery. They each carried an armful of petunias, geraniums, and many other flowers.

They stopped at Holly's headstone and Michelle lay the flowers down.

"Thank you, Holly," she said. "Some people may have said you were a bad influence on me, but I loved you. Sometimes I may have hated you, but I grew because of you. I wouldn't be who I am today if it weren't for you. And having known you will help me raise my own children better. I'll be a better parent – because I know what they'll go through. Thank you for saving me – AGAIN!"

As they passed by a lilac bush, they saw a gravestone with a fresh flower arrangement covering the grass in front. They knew whose grave it was without reading the name – Billy Kinecki's. And they knew who left the arrangement – the centerpiece was a blue Teddy Bear.

AUTHOR'S NOTES

Many influences and ideas went into this story. I get the sense that if my life hadn't ended up exactly where it is today – for better or worse – this book wouldn't have come out the way it did.

The first was a mysterious accident that happened close to where I used to live. The building where it happened took on an aura, and as the years went by, I wondered more and more what really happened. When I finally researched it over twenty years later, I found out some very disturbing facts. I also received two threats, one of them a death threat, if I were to ask any more questions. The death threat came from a wealthy, powerful man who is rumored to have underworld ties.

The incident may have been a police cover up, and the police in the town where I used to live harassed me, causing me to lose my business. So I went bankrupt. That was about the time I started writing this.

My family experienced a similar tragedy, although it wasn't drug or alcohol related. The girl who would have been my aunt died from a disease at 15. This deeply affects our family, even to this day.

I was an avid user of drugs when I was 16. Then I realized they were destroying me, so I decided to quit. I saw the darker side of life. Several of my former friends ended up in jail, or in drug rehab, or dead, or all of the above.

I know what it's like to be picked on and ridiculed. Having a slight physical handicap made me an easy target when I was a kid.

I taught high school for 11 years. That gave me an understanding of the teenage mind. Times may change, but human nature doesn't.

One of my best friends lived at a home for troubled teens and I spent many hours there hanging out with him. Though difficult at times, this was a valuable study in dysfunctional teenage behavior.

I read an article once in a detective magazine about two teenage boys who went into the woods and took LSD. One boy ran headfirst into a tree and was killed. His friend buried him by the bank of a river, but they never found the body because the mud settled. With no body, the friend was never charged with a crime!

Many years ago, in our town, a young teacher was murdered. The milkman found the body and confessed to the crime, even though the police knew he didn't do it. He loved her, and he felt so bad about it that he wanted to punish himself!

Finally, the *Scooby Doo* cartoons always had a great summary at the end that explained the mystery and left no loose ends. It was always a logical explanation, and not some alien life form or supernatural being. I like endings like that.

This book may disturb some people, but I realized as I was writing it that I can't make everybody happy. I can only write what comes from my heart. If you like it, great. If not, read something else! But please keep reading *something*, every day. Not enough people do.

For better or worse, I really enjoyed writing this. No matter what happens, I am very proud of it. And if you liked it, let's meet for coffee sometime! - R.M. Wood